W9-DBQ-836

FUNERAL AT NOON

FUNERAL AT NOON

YESHAYAHU KOREN

TRANSLATED BY DALYA BILU

STEERFORTH PRESS

South Royalton, Vermont

For information about permission to reproduce selections from this
book, write to: Steerforth Press L.C., P.O. Box 70, South Royalton,
Vermont 05068.

First published in Hebrew in 1974 by Siman Kriah, Tel Aviv.

Library of Congress Cataloging-in-Publication Data

Koren, Yeshayahu.
    [Levayah ba-tsohorayim.   English]
    Funeral at noon / Yeshayahu Koren ; [translated by
    Dalya Bilu].
       p. cm.
    ISBN 1-883642-03-5 (alk. paper)
    I. Bilu, Dalya. II. Title.
 PJ5054.K578L4813   1996
  892.4 ' 36--dc20   95-48321   CIP

Manufactured in the United States of America

FIRST EDITION

PART ONE

I

Hagar Erlich was sitting on the veranda overlooking the deserted Arab village. An open magazine was lying on the floor next to the round, wooden legs of her chair. She sat looking around her. Among the houses of the ruined village she suddenly noticed a platoon of soldiers. There were packs on their backs. They were walking in a long line.

It was noon. She went into the kitchen, opened the refrigerator and took out an apple. Then she picked up a knife and began to peel it. The dishes in the sink were unwashed. "I have to make lunch," she said to herself, stood up, and went into the bathroom. She looked in the mirror and smoothed down her hair. Her face was narrow, her lashes sparse. But her green eyes still flashed with a restless flicker. There were already a few lines on her forehead.

"What's happened to him today?"

Again she went out to the veranda. In the distance she heard the chugging of a jeep. "Maybe that's him?"

But the jeep didn't turn into the street and the chugging died away.

She walked to the bottom of the yard. The mailbox on the gate was empty. A truck loaded with watermelons drove down the street. A boy in a T-shirt was sitting on top of the pile and holding onto the slats of the frame.

Dry gray grass stretched out along the roadside. She got dressed, took a basket, and went out.

In the grocery store there were several women standing in line. Hagar waited next to the window and looked at Kasos's cafe. The cafe served as a restaurant too. It was the only restaurant in the colony, and for the first time she noticed the writing on the wall above the wide entrance, in faded brown paint: "Moshe Kasos. Shady Pines." The letters had peeled along with the whitewash flaking off the walls. There wasn't a pine in sight. But next to the restaurant was an empty lot strewn with old tires, crates and sawed-off planks. In front of the restaurant, at the edge of the pavement, grew a Pride of India tree. There was a bicycle leaning against its trunk, and two boys came out of the cafe, licking ice cream cones.

"Afternoon, Mrs. Erlich," said Tabak, the grocer. It was her turn.

When she came out of the grocer's she went into Kasos's cafe and bought a glass of juice. Kasos greeted her, stared at her, and dropped his eyes.

"Is anything wrong?" she asked him.

"No, nothing," he said. "It's hot today."

He had a white apron on and he was holding a wet cloth in his hand. Two workers in dirty blue overalls were standing at the counter drinking beer. There were beads of sweat on Kasos's forehead. His eyes were lowered and although the marble was smooth and shining, he slid the wet cloth over it. Hagar put her glass down on the counter, paid, and went outside.

The basket was heavy and her feet sank into the sand. A dry leaf got into one of her flat shoes. A fence made of wooden poles ran across the open field opposite her. The houses in the street were isolated, far apart, orphaned.

As she walked into the yard the last of the soldiers left the Arab village and disappeared in the orange groves.

On the kitchen windowsill, under a can of nails, the key was hidden. She went inside and opened the shutters.

The light splashing into the house brought a chilly breath of air with it. She changed her dress and went out again. She walked toward the ruined Arab village. Three spreading olive trees stood at the entrance to the village. A wide, flat gray rock pressed against one of their trunks.

The sun was about to sink. Its flat rays filtered through the olive branches, hit the shutterless windows, and accentuated the darkness which had gathered in the empty rooms.

She wandered through the narrow streets, where the smell of the outdoor ovens still lingered, and came to the well. The troughs were full of water. An old pail, tied to a rope, lay on its side on the paving stones bordering the well. There was smoke rising from one of the courtyards. She approached and saw a heap of dying embers in the yard. Empty cans were strewn among the embers and there were cigarette ends lying next to a stone wall. She walked along the wall and her hands slid over the stones. Opposite a low ruin there was a gap in the wall and next to it she saw something glittering. When she came closer to the object, her shadow fell on it and the glitter disappeared. It was an open canteen. She picked it up, holding it by its narrow steel chain, and left the village.

When she walked past the olive trees again, she tore a slender branch off one of them. The sun had already set. Only the horizon still retained the vestiges of the dying day. The path where she was walking was full of grass, and low, dry thorns scratched her legs. The path led her to the main road. The red horizon grew gray and a breeze brushed the smooth asphalt. Suddenly she felt ashamed of the canteen she had found, and whenever the headlights of a car shone on her she hid it behind her back.

When she approached their yard she saw that her husband's jeep was parked next to the gate, and there was a light on in the kitchen.

The wind came up and rustled the leaves. She threw away the olive switch and slowly climbed the steps of the veranda in front of the kitchen, went up to the narrow cupboard built into the wall, and put the canteen inside it. The door creaked when she shut it and she started. There was no reaction from the kitchen. She smoothed her hair back with both hands and went inside.

2

Her husband was sitting at the table reading the newspaper. In front of him was the cup of coffee he had made himself.

"Hello," she said.

"Yes?" said her husband.

There was a knock at the kitchen door.

She turned around. "Who's there?" she asked.

There was no reply. The knocking at the door continued. It was faint and rhythmic.

Her husband stood up, took a sip of the coffee which was no longer steaming, and went to the door.

"Who's there?" He opened the door.

Yiftach was standing in the doorway. He was a child of about ten, short, with a round face and straight yellow hair. The son of Sarah and Simcha Strauss, their neighbors who lived across the street. He was wearing brown sandals, short gym pants, and a thin, sloppy shirt. In his hand was an empty glass jar.

Her husband sat down and took another sip of coffee. Hagar remained standing next to the door.

"Hello," he said quietly.

"Hello," she said.

The child advanced from the door to the table.

"Did you want something?" she asked.

"My mother wants to know if you can let us have a bit of salt. She forgot to buy any and all the salt's finished."

The child held out the jar and she put it down on the marble counter next to the sink. She opened the door of the cupboard hanging on the wall and took out a broad square box. Then she took a spoon out of the sink, turned on the tap and washed it. As she wiped it dry, she asked the child: "Do you want a sweet?"

"My mother wants to know if you can let us have a bit of salt," Yiftach said again.

"And you, don't you want a sweet?"

With the dry spoon she transferred salt from the tin to the child's jar. Then she went to the brown chest under the window and opened one of its drawers. She took out a red glass dish and removed the lid.

The dish was empty. "I'm sorry," she said softly, "there aren't any sweets left."

"Thanks for the salt," said the child and turned toward the door.

There was a grain of salt sticking to Hagar's hand.

They could hear the child's muffled footsteps in the sand. Her husband finished drinking his cold coffee, and she began washing the dishes and put the kettle on the gas. The water hit the saucepans and dishes in the sink, spraying clear drops on her dress. She listened to the water splashing into the sink and heard her husband's footsteps. He went to the bathroom.

She dried the dishes and put them away in the cupboard. Then she went to the bedroom and took a clean pair of socks, a white shirt, and pressed trousers out of the wardrobe.

"I've brought your clothes." She stood outside the bathroom door.

The water stopped splashing. The clatter of his clogs approached the door and his sinewy hand emerged.

"I brought you a change of clothes," she said. Water dripped from his hand to the floor.

"Thanks." The door closed again.

When she returned to the kitchen she heard the water running in the shower again. There were no more dishes left in the sink, and she cut up the fish and put the frying pan on the gas.

The plates were on the table and she was slicing the bread when her husband appeared in the doorway, shaved, his wet hair combed.

He smiled.

A smell of garlic, onions, olives, and tomatoes rose from the pan.

Her eyes were fixed on her plate and he buttered himself a slice of bread. Her fork clattered on her plate. The rustle of leaves rose from the yard and came in through the open windows.

"Did we get any letters today?" he asked.

"No. Who were you expecting one from?"

"I was just asking."

"Why didn't you come home for lunch?"

"Why do you ask?"

"I was afraid."

"What of?"

"Did you have anything to eat?"

"Yes."

"Where?"

"I have to go and see Yoel. Today's Thursday. There are problems at the garage. Nobody pays cash and we're up to our necks already."

"It's hot. Would you like to go to the sea on Saturday?"

"Sure."

"And where did you have lunch today?"

"At Kasos's."

"I thought you had a lot of work."

"We did have a lot of work."

"Shady Pines," she said.

"What did you say?"

"Shady Pines."

"What's that?"

"It's the name of Kasos's cafe."

"How do you know?"

"It's painted on the wall, in brown paint."

"I've never seen it there."

"Yes, the paint's peeling. Parts of the letters are missing."

It was eight-thirty. Her husband drove off to see his partner, Yoel. The house was too quiet. Hagar turned on the radio and went to wash. When she entered the bedroom again she looked at their wedding photograph, which was hanging on the wall. She turned down the covers of the bed, took a book from the bookcase, and lay down under the thin blanket.

Outside the warm wind caressed the walls. Hagar heard a car engine and a yellow jet of light pierced the shutter, crossed the wall and disappeared. She couldn't read. She put the book down next to the reading lamp and fell asleep.

3

On Friday afternoon she again sat on the veranda and watched the Arab village. And on Saturday too, when they got back from the sea. But it was only on Sunday, after lunch, that she saw them again. Appearing and disappearing between the ruined houses. A platoon of soldiers. Wearing packs and steel helmets.

She left the veranda and walked to the gate. At the end of the road she saw three women wearing long dresses with scarves on their heads. They turned left, to the square.

She went back inside and changed into a long, green dress with black buttons all the way down the front. Then she took out of the wardrobe a skein of wool, knitting needles, and the back of a sweater she had once begun knitting for her husband. She put the ball of wool into an embroidered bag, tied a scarf round her head, and went into the street.

In the square between Tabak's grocery store and Kasos's cafe few cars were parked, and the solitary man leaning on the cafe counter only served to emphasize the desolation surrounding him. But the main street was crowded with people, and the shops, although they were open, were deserted. On the gray trunks of the ficus trees she saw the reason. Black mourning notices were pinned to the tree trunks. Esther Schmerling, the teacher, was dead.

Next to the synagogue, opposite the council house, a large crowd had gathered, making a wide circle in the center of which stood the hearse. The head of the mare harnessed to the wagon was lowered. Her white coat was dappled with gray spots and patches. There was an iron bit in her mouth, and the reins leading from it were wrapped around the carved wooden post sticking up at the edge of the driver's seat.

Friedman, the cart-driver, stood next to the mare. His short beard had turned white, but the sailor's cap on his head cast a dark gray shadow over it.

The headmaster of the school spoke. The teachers hushed the children, who were lined up in straggling rows. The girls carried bunches of flowers. The boys wore blue uniform shirts. Occasionally a mother went up to her son. The teachers would intervene and try to restore order.

"Esther was a good woman." The headmaster repeated this comment several times. Esther Schmerling's son, who worked as a gardener at the school, leaned against the black wagon. Friedman, his hands outspread, his head bowed, stood next to him. A number of men, wearing hats or flat peaked caps, stood behind them. Kasos's wife stood with them. The other women stood to the side, next to the schoolchildren.

"Esther was a good woman." Hagar Erlich did not mingle with the mourners. She looked at the dome of the synagogue and the two eucalyptus trees bowed over the roof; she heard the murmurs of the crowd accompanying the headmaster's voice.

The funeral procession left the synagogue yard and passed the council house with the little dormer windows jutting out of its red tiled roof. Once these had served as attics and latticed window-chimneys in the days of the Turks. The yard was full of faded trees, pines which had shed their needles.

At the head of the procession loomed Friedman's black sea captain's cap. Hagar Erlich brought up the rear.

A dirt road crossed the main street and the funeral procession turned into it.

On the right of the dirt road was an open field, full of thorns. On the left, an orange grove. A smell of wet earth rose from it. The irrigation was on, and tiny mosquitoes flew into the procession in airy little swarms.

"She was still young," said the skinny woman walking in front of Hagar.

"How old was she?" a second woman asked.

"Fifty-one."

"When did they discover it?"

"Last summer."

"And why didn't they treat her?"

"They did. But it was hopeless. She knew."

"Did she go on teaching?"

"Yes."

They reached the cemetery, which lay between an orange grove and a little orchard. The plums and apricots were not yet ripe, only the loquat tree spread a dry smell around it. The school building could be seen not far off, separated from the cemetery by a plowed field.

Children ran into the orchard to pick the fruit. Their teachers ran after them.

"In winter it rains," thought Hagar, "and the trees are bare. In summer it's hot and the air burns. How come the fruit ripens in summer?" She giggled to herself. The children came back from the orchard empty handed.

They entered the cemetery. Between the gravestones were pine trees, cypresses and flowers. Hagar remained standing behind the fence.

Among the men throwing earth into the grave she saw Yoel, her husband's partner. He threw a few spadefuls of earth into the pit, handed the spade to someone else, and rejoined the crowd. An old woman left the crowd clustering around the grave and wandered off among the gravestones.

Hagar stood next to the fence. Yoel came up to her.

"Why didn't Tuvia come?"

"He knew that you would come, and someone had to stay in the garage."

"Where's your wife?"

"The girl's sick. Carmela had to stay with her."

"She could have stayed home with Ronny."

"Ronny's here. He was in Esther's class."

"Really?"

Someone delivered a eulogy. One of her colleagues, a man. Yoel resumed his place among the other mourners. His son stepped out of the line of children and came up to him. Yoel put out his hand and they stood in silence, holding hands. Hagar's hands gripped the fence. The old woman who had left the crowd came to a halt next to a grave at the side of the cemetery, bent down and placed a stone on the white gravestone.

Hagar let go of the fence and walked away. She walked along the orange grove with a swarm of mosquitoes following her like a cloud. Occasionally a mosquito would dive for her forehead and she would chase it away with a wave of her hand. A smell of rotten oranges rose into her nostrils, and only the splashing of water in the irrigation canals evoked an image of living trees.

When she reached the main road she took the scarf off her head. To her left the road continued to the shops and the square. To her right – to the ruined Arab village. In the middle of the open field in front of her was a narrow path. A solitary donkey, tethered to the stump of a tree, was grazing on the grass. She stepped onto the path and walked toward the village.

The knitting bag dragged on her arm. She was thirsty. Even the donkey stopped chewing the grass. Flies collected in the ooze surrounding its big, moist eyes. Its mouth was open and its tongue hung out. The rope, plaited like a braid, dangled from its neck and twisted on the ground.

A dry bush stuck to her skirt, and when she thrust it away it scratched her fingers. But by then she was already in the shade of the olive trees. The rock lying beneath them was cool and shady. She sat down on it and her thirst passed.

Voices echoed between the houses. The soldiers left the village and marched north. The packs on their backs bowed their shoulders. She stopped knitting. The soldiers leaned on the long stone wall and kept their eyes on the ground. She couldn't see their faces. From the back they were all alike. High black boots, patched khaki trousers, backpack, spade, rifle barrel, steel helmet.

There was a sound of ringing metal. She raised her head, but she couldn't see anything. But when she put her knitting away in her bag she saw hobbling feet. A solitary soldier emerged from the village. He was limping and dragging his foot over the stones. He too walked along the wall. He too had a backpack, a steel helmet and a gun. He followed the other soldiers. Suddenly he stopped and leaned against the wall. His back was to the olive trees beneath which Hagar was sitting. There was a streak of white salt on his shirt, in the small of his back.

The sun had already gone down. The soldier's face was wet with sweat. His helmet lay at his feet, on the ground, and his hair was plastered to his forehead. His nose was humped. He raised his hand to his forehead and wiped the sweat off. Then he bent down and took off his left boot. His foot was bandaged. He removed the bandage and, with a handkerchief he took out of his pocket, he cleaned the wound. Then he bandaged his foot again and put on his boot. Before setting out he turned around. He saw her, but he turned around again and limped after the platoon.

Hagar watched his dragging foot. Like the others, he too walked with his back bowed, his eyes on the ground. He disappeared from view, leaving the stone wall deserted. She picked up her knitting bag, tied the scarf around her head, and started walking back through the field. The donkey was still there, and only the braided rope had changed its position among the grass and thorns. The sun touched the roofs of the ruined houses and Hagar felt thirsty again. When she reached the main street, she went into Tabak's grocery store, bought a few things, wrapped them up, and put them into her knitting bag.

In Kasos's cafe steaming bowls of soup stood in the passage connecting the kitchen with the restaurant. On the doorstep at the entrance stood Noah Bulkin. His heavy shadow lay on the road, as if bisecting it. His boots were caked with mud.

In the evening, while she was cooking, Yiftach, Sarah and Simcha Strauss's son, came again. He brought a few meatballs and a piquant sauce. "Mother wants you to taste this," he said. She gave him some of the sweets she had bought at Tabak's, and he left.

Tuvia, her husband, came home tired.

"There's a pile of accounts to do," he said, "but I haven't got the strength. Do you want to go to the movies?"

They went after supper.

During the intermission, people in the row behind them were talking about Esther Schmerling.

"Who're they going to get to replace her?"

"It's no good for the children, all this chopping and changing."

At midnight they went to bed. The bedroom shutters were open and a pleasant summery coolness came into the room. In the morning, with the weak light of the rising sun, the coolness turned into a bracing chill and at half past six the alarm clock went off.

4

The fingernails scratched at the wall.

The soft fingers were misshapen.

He knelt with his chest and face pressed against the whitewash. His hands beat the wall and scratched it. Sometimes he fell to the ground, lay flat on the floor, and wept soundlessly. And his soft, white nails tried to scratch signs in the whitewash.

His nose was broad, stuck to his mouth. His forehead was big and smooth, taking up half his head. The black eyes were small, tiny. They saw nothing. He crawled along the wall, and the hands stretched out in front of him beat the floor, trying to scratch it too.

Torn paper bags were strewn around the room. Toys, leftover food.

He went on crawling along the wall and reached the door. The door was closed and he threw himself against the wood. The door did not open, and he raised himself to his knees again, scratched the dry wood and banged his head against it. Dull thuds echoed from the door and he fell down again, his blind eyes closed and squeezed shut, his face crumpled. He wept. But there was no sound.

Curled into a ball, like a hedgehog without spines, he lay on the floor, pressed against the door.

The door opened.

On the doorstep stood Yiftach. His toes tapped his brown sandals. He was wearing blue gym shorts and a T-shirt, and he looked at his baby brother. The door had opened so suddenly that the human ball fell outside, onto the step where Yiftach was standing. The heat outside roused him. Again he lay flat on his stomach, and stretched his hands out in front of him. But there was no wall or door in front of him. His fingers scratched the air.

Yiftach recoiled. He wanted to scream, but his baby brother had already fallen off the step onto the sand. He stretched himself and began to crawl. His fingers hidden in the sand, digging into it, he advanced. His pants were full of sand. For a moment he tired and bowed his head. Yiftach watched the head turning toward the empty blue sky, cloudless and windless.

Then he went on crawling toward the fence and got into the thorn patch. His fingers clutched a dry bush. Drops of blood oozed from his pale skin. He curled up and his face twisted. Yiftach went up to him. He wanted to pick him up, but instead he shouted: "Ma!"

Their mother was in the toolshed. She was doing the laundry. There were already sheets, towels, underwear, and diapers hanging on the clothesline. She didn't hear his shout. The big tap was on. The water splashed onto the clothes in the sink, and she fed the stove under the cauldron of water with fresh wood. The embers whispered and the wood, when the fire caught it, snapped convulsively.

The baby clung to the thornbush and Yiftach did not call his mother again. He picked his brother up, and went back to the house with him.

In the bathroom he undressed him, and threw his clothes into the laundry hamper. Then he put him in a hot bath and tried to pull out the thorns sticking into his flesh. The drops of blood disappeared. The baby stopped crying. His eyes were closed, and it seemed to Yiftach that he was sleeping. He wrapped clean diapers around him and carried him in his arms to the bed. He covered him with a light blanket, closed the shutters and the window, left the room and went into the kitchen. His forehead was bathed in sweat. He went over to the sink and washed his face.

From the window he saw smoke rising from the shed in the yard and his mother bending over the tub in the dim interior. Next to the fence were fruit trees. Along the sides of the path winding to the toolshed grew dry, thorny weeds. Drops of water fell from the edges of the laundry hanging on the line. In the middle of the yard, next to a solitary iron pole, lay a big wooden box full of old toys and rusty nails.

When he reached the door to the toolshed his mother came out with a basin full of wrung-out laundry in her hands.

"Just a minute," she said to him, and he stepped off the path and stood in the thorns.

The smell of burning wood rose in his nostrils. His mother put the basin on the ground and took some clothespins out of her apron pocket.

Yiftach followed her and stood next to the iron pole, his hand resting on the side of the high wooden box.

"Just a minute," she said, "just let me finish hanging it out."

He took his hand off the box and leaned against the pole.

"Will you go to the store?"

"Okay," he said, "but he got out again."

"Where?" Her hand, straightening an undershirt on the line, froze.

"Outside, in the thorns."

"Why didn't you call me?" She clipped a pin onto the line.

"You didn't hear."

"You should have called me."

She finished hanging up the laundry, picked up the basin, and returned to the toolshed.

"What's he doing now?"

"Sleeping."

She took off her apron and hung it on the wall. Under the cauldron the flames had died down.

"Good, I'm going to see how he is. And you go to the store."

He walked down the path behind her.

"What should I get?"

"The same as always. And get two kilos of rice too."

Yiftach went into the kitchen, took the basket, and set out. His mother went into the dark room where his little brother was sleeping.

When he got back his mother wasn't there. He put the basket down on a low bench in the kitchen, drank a glass of cold water, and cut himself a slice of bread from the loaf he had just bought. Then he heard the wooden gate creaking and his mother's footsteps.

"Did you get everything?"

"Yes. Here's the change." He pulled a few coins from his pocket and scattered them on the table cloth.

"I went over to Hagar's," she said. "I'm taking him to see the doctor again."

"Okay."

She went into the bedroom. The wardrobe doors creaked as they opened and shut. When she emerged from the room she was wearing a green summer dress, and her low heels tapped on the floor. Her hair was bound up in a scarf. In front of the mirror she removed the scarf and let her hair fall to her shoulders. As she did so she said: "If you need anything go to her."

"I don't need anything."

"She's going out this afternoon. I asked her to take you with her. I'll be back late. Daddy too. Go with her."

He leaned with his back against the wall, his legs crossed.

"You can play with the kids in the street too. But I want you to go to her for supper. She suggested it herself."

"Okay."

She finished fixing her hair and making up her face and came out of the bathroom. She wrapped his little brother in a blanket and picked him up. Her brown leather bag was slung over her shoulder.

She left the house and Yiftach remained in the kitchen, staring at the closed shutter. Then he suddenly stood up, opened the door, and ran after his mother. She was no longer in the street and all he could see were her footprints in the sand. On the main road, he caught up with her.

She heard him panting and asked, "What happened?"

"I decided to come with you to the bus stop."

She gave him her bag and he walked beside her. Next to the bus stop they stopped.

There were beads of sweat on his mother's forehead. Trucks and a cart drawn by a donkey passed them on the road. A few people stood at the counter of Kasos's cafe.

"It's hot," said his mother. "Open my bag and take out a few *grosch* for soda."

By the time he had finished rummaging in her purse the bus was already at the stop. With her free hand his mother rumpled his hair.

"You need a haircut," she said and climbed onto the bus. The door shut behind her. The bus drove off. He stood there and watched her standing next to the driver as he gave her a ticket.

In Kasos's cafe Yiftach asked for a soda. He held the cold glass in his hands and looked at the two workers standing next to him drinking beer.

"Put on some music, Kasos," said one of them to Kasos who was wiping the counter with a wet cloth. "Maybe it'll cool us down."

"Okay, I'll put on a bit of music," said Kasos, "but don't expect it to dry your sweat."

"Never mind if it does or it doesn't, I'm dried to a frazzle already."

Kasos topped up the worker's glass and then went over to the gramophone.

A tired Spanish song filled the cafe, and Yiftach sipped his soda and looked at the black-and-white photograph hanging on the wall. The landscape in the photograph was a familiar one: a solitary house with a tall pine tree leaning over its tiled roof, and the facade of a cafe. On the wall, in curly black letters – "Shady Pines." Kasos's cafe.

"Did you want anything else, kid?" Kasos came up to him, picked up his empty glass, and wiped the gray marble.

"No," said Yiftach. Again he glanced at the gray

photograph, and with the Spanish singer whistling in his ears he left the cafe.

An old man was whitewashing the trunks of the eucalyptus trees in whose shade Yiftach was walking.

The empty lot opposite their house was deserted. He opened the wooden gate, saw the laundry drying on the long wire lines, and went inside.

He threw his shirt onto a chair, lay down, and tried to fall asleep.

Suddenly he heard the wooden gate opening. There was a knock at the door.

"Who's there?" he asked.

He heard two more knocks.

He got off the bed, put on his shirt and sandals, and went to the door.

"Who's there?"

When he took hold of the handle he felt someone else holding it on the other side. The door opened and he saw Hagar. She was wearing a green sleeveless dress. She was wearing sandals too.

"Aren't you lonely by yourself?" she asked.

"No," he said.

"It's hot out."

"I know."

"Come home with me," she said. "I've got some ice cream for you."

"I don't like ice cream."

"But I've got lemonade and plum jam too."

"I have to do my homework."

"Good, so finish it first. But come afterward, all right?"

Hagar came into the kitchen. "Should I make you something to eat now?"

"There's no need. Actually, I'll come with you, if you like."

"And you haven't got homework?"

"No. It's the end of term, our teacher's stopped giving us homework."

When they went out into the yard the oppressive heat had lightened a little. The laundry hung helplessly on the line. The shirt sleeves flapped limply, as if asking to be rescued. In the distance the air was hazy, like the mist in winter. It covered the cypresses hedging the orange grove and dulled the color of the ruined houses in the abandoned Arab village. They walked toward the gate and then Yiftach, as if remembering something, said: "I think the laundry has to be taken down."

They returned to the toolshed. The fire was out. A burned smell, mixed with the smell of a dark, closed place and of laundry soap, hung in the air. Hagar took an empty basin and went outside. She plucked the dry laundry from the line and Yiftach walked behind her collecting the clothespins.

Then they crossed the dirt road and went into Hagar's house.

She served the ice cream. He sat at the table and said nothing. From the lot rose the cries of children playing soccer. She went into the hall and switched on the radio. When she came back Yiftach's dish was empty.

"Do you want some more?"

"No."

"Are you thirsty?"

He didn't answer. She took the lemonade out of the refrigerator and poured him a glass, and in another dish she put jam and a teaspoon. Then she left him alone and went into the bathroom. When she came out she was wearing a yellow dress. In her hand she held the knitting bag. Yiftach stood up and walked around the kitchen.

"Shall we go?" she said, and put the bag down on the table.

Yiftach heard the shutters opening and breathed in the fresh air. Through one of the windows he saw the children running in the empty lot.

"Where should we go?"

They were on the road, walking in the direction of the Arab village. In the distance it looked desolate, blurred. The trees in the open field looked bowed too. Only their summits were lighter, sending out pale leaves to the high, clear air.

"Where should we go?" she asked again. But they were already in the field. The air cleared and the houses in the village opposite them took on shape and color. Only the distant mountains, the mountains behind the white houses of the *moshav**, were shrouded in a haze of fine dust. Along the paved road in the middle of the village trundled a donkey cart. Beneath the olive trees, on the broad rock, sat a soldier, his back leaning against the tree trunk, his gun propped against his body. His backpack and helmet lay on the ground.

---

*A cooperative smallholders' settlement

"You see that soldier?" she asked.

"The one sitting next to the tree?"

"What, are there more of them?"

"Can't you see? They're walking next to the orange grove, in a line. Look, the first one's already gone into the grove. And now the second one's gone in too."

"Yes, I see them."

"And why's that one sitting by the tree?"

"So you see him?"

"Yes."

"Once he lost his canteen."

"How do you know?"

The sun was behind them. Their shadows stretched out on the ground, creeping ahead of them. To Yiftach the shadows seemed to be leading them, while they pursued. He looked at the soldiers entering the orange grove and disappearing into it one by one, and then his eyes traveled over the stone wall bordering the village until they reached the spreading olive trees and the soldier sitting next to them.

"How do you know?" he asked again.

She was walking beside him. Her shadow, climbing over the grass and the thorny bushes, writhed and sometimes seemed to break. The path along which they walked was narrow, and in order to keep Yiftach's feet from being scratched by the thorns, she walked through them herself. When she encountered a bigger bush, she too was obliged to step onto the path. Then they walked close together, and their shadows merged, turning into one rough body crawling over the thorns.

"He's always the last, that soldier," she said.

"The one sitting next to the tree?"

"Yes, they walk a lot, those soldiers."

"They're soldiers, aren't they?"

"I always see that soldier. He's always last. First he has to rest, and then he gets up and follows behind all the others."

"So he's not a good soldier."

The path led to the olive trees. But they made a detour around the trees, crossed a bare plot of ground, and entered the village. They walked between the houses and Yiftach ran his hand over the stone and mortar walls. Bits of straw poked out between the stones. There was straw scattered over the sand they were walking on too. They went through an arched doorway into a house. The entrance hall was paved with concrete, and the floor was covered with sand and dust. From the entrance, openings led in all directions, some straight and rectangular, some arched. On their left was a wide doorway with a row of dark stones arched above it. There were leaves and jars carved in the arch. Some of the grooves were still painted black, the others were pale and colorless. The row of stones ran down to the floor in the shape of a horseshoe. There was a smell of mold inside, but Yiftach put his hand on the stones and said: "It's cold, this horseshoe."

Stepping through the horseshoe-door they entered a big room. It had two high windows in it, their slender bars studded with wrought iron flowers. The paint had peeled from the walls. Only high up next to the ceiling were traces of the blue paint still visible, together with a red line marking the border between the walls and the ceiling. The ceiling too was cracked, and pale shafts of light filtered through the cracks into the room. The shafts of light were thick with tiny motes of dust. One ray of light lay on the step in the corner of the room.

Hagar stood next to the barred window. The house opposite her was a ruin, and through the broken walls she could see the olive trees and the soldier's stretched-out legs. His boots were nailed and scuffed. She couldn't see his body. Nor the rock on which he was sitting. His legs seemed to be suspended in the air.

Next to the step illumined by the ray of light Yiftach leaned against the wall. A chill penetrated his thin shirt. He looked at the step. A narrow stairway wound upward from it. The stairs led him to a second floor. This consisted of a small room with a single window, round and unbarred, like a porthole. The blue paint here was intact, but the smell of mold was worse. He left the room and went on climbing the steps, which led to the roof. He stood on the roof and looked down at the abandoned village.

Hagar looked at the soldier's legs, stretched motionless in front of him. Then she turned around. She couldn't see Yiftach.

"Yiftach," she called and went outside.

She returned to the house. "Yiftach," she called into the empty room.

Only then did she see the illuminated step. She climbed the steps to the little room, and when she didn't find him there either, she went on climbing.

"I didn't know where you'd disappeared to," she said to him. "I was afraid you'd run away."

He sat cross-legged on the domed roof. His arms were folded on his knees.

"You can see everything from here," he said, "even the soldier."

They looked down on the dry field. The last houses of the colony. The eucalyptus trees and the main road. They watched the green bus leaving the bus station and disappearing behind the hill. The rows of houses were divided into square blocks by the streets and roads. Only here and there, on the outskirts, were houses with big yards and fences.

Around them lay the Arab village, a cluster of brown houses and collapsing walls. Winding streets of sand and stone, and a flat square with a well in its center. Stone fences joined up to the walls of the houses. Opposite them was a tumbledown fence. Inside the village, along the edges of the dirt road, weeds and thorns climbed the walls. An empty tin can glinted among them.

They took one step down and looked at the mountains which as evening fell had suddenly grown clearer. The Arab villages clinging to the mountainside looked like masses of darkness, and the only sign of life to be seen were the trees and the white-domed sepulchres. For the *moshav* on the other side of the road was deserted too. Only the watchman's dog could be seen, running along the wall.

Hagar went on looking at the mountains, and Yiftach said: "Look, the soldier's started walking."

Limping, he left the shade of the olive trees and dragged himself along the stone fence.

"There's a canteen on his webbing," said Yiftach.

"I'm sure he lost his canteen," said Hagar.

"How do you know?"

They went down the stairs and left the house through the horseshoe-shaped door.

"I found it," she said.

"Where?"

"Here, between the stones, next to the well."

Yiftach went first. They walked in the direction of the orange grove.

"Don't run," she said. "I can't keep up." She stumbled on a stone.

"Where's the canteen now?"

"In my house," she panted. "Don't run."

"Will you give it to me?"

Yiftach slowed down, and Hagar caught up with him. They walked side by side, the child on the path and she on the stony ground next to it. Again his steps grew quicker, and when he saw that she was stumbling he stepped off the path and walked between the stones. He slowed down, and she moved onto the path and caught up with him.

"Were you in Esther Schmerling's class?" she asked him suddenly.

"No, why do you want to know?"

"Once I studied to be a teacher too."

"Are you a teacher?"

"No. I never completed my studies. I could have been a teacher at your school."

"Will you be my teacher?"

They were next to the wall. Behind it began the orange grove. The soldier, walking along the wall, was about ten paces in front of them. Yiftach began walking quickly again. Hagar looked at the straps of the pack on the soldier's back, at the steel helmet dangling from his hand, at his bowed head.

"Hey, soldier," called Yiftach.

The soldier stopped, leaned on the fence, and smiled. He leaned on his gun, as if it were a walking stick.

"Don't you have to catch up with the other soldiers?"

"Yes," said the soldier.

"So get a move on," urged Yiftach.

The soldier walked on the path, next to the fence. Hagar and Yiftach walked next to him, on the grass and the stones.

Hagar's eyes examined the soldier's face. His hair was uncut. Uncombed as well. Dry sweat ran in dark, narrow streaks down his cheeks, like a continuation of his sideburns. His hair was straight and brown, stuck to his head, with one lock plastered to his forehead. His nose was a little crooked, drooping down toward his thick lips. His mouth was closed. Around the canteen, on his trousers, was a dark stain of water.

"Was it you who lost the canteen?" asked Yiftach.

"What canteen?"

"I found a canteen here a few days ago," said Hagar.

"I've got a canteen," said the soldier.

"A few days ago. Wasn't it you? I saw a soldier, just like you. Sitting next to the olive trees. Then he got up and followed the platoon. He was limping too."

"Every day a different soldier limps and brings up the rear."

"So it wasn't you?"

"I twisted my ankle today, in training."

"Is your camp far?" asked Yiftach.

"So-so."

"How do you get there? On foot?"

"No. There's a truck waiting for us on the other side of the orange grove."

"Right," said Yiftach. "I saw it from the roof of the house."

"Maybe next time I'll bring you the canteen," said Hagar.

"But I never lost any canteen," said the soldier.

"Then you can return it to whoever did lose it," she said.

"Is it a long way to the other side of the orange grove?" asked Yiftach.

"Not so long."

"The other soldiers are waiting for you," said Yiftach.

The soldier was silent.

"Should we come with you?"

The soldier smiled.

"I'm thirsty," said Yiftach.

Suddenly the soldier quickened his pace.

The sun disappeared and the roofs of the colony became sharp, colorless silhouettes. The child, the woman, and the soldier went into the orange grove.

5

"If he doesn't want to take the canteen will you give it to me?"

They were on the way back. The light was dying, they no longer saw the sun. The air grew clear as night began to fall, and in the distance, on the dirt track, a cloud of dust rose in the wake of the army truck.

They walked on the path alongside the orange grove. When they reached the end they saw a weak light shining from the window of a solitary house. Surrounding the house was a yard with fruit trees, a cow shed, and a large henhouse.

"That's Noah Bulkin's house," said Yiftach.

"I know," said Hagar.

"What does he do here alone all day?"

"He works."

The lights were already on in the colony. As they approached they saw Noah Bulkin coming up the road. He had a knapsack slung over his shoulder and a flat cap on his head. His shirtsleeves were rolled up, his arms were hairy. He greeted them, and they continued on their way.

"Once I went to his house," said Yiftach. "My dad fixed the electricity in his henhouse. It's a funny house. It's got three rooms and only one bed."

"In Kasos's cafe he always eats alone too," said Hagar.

Yiftach's house was still in darkness.

"Your mother isn't home yet," said Hagar.

"My dad either," said Yiftach.

"You'll have supper with us," said Hagar.

"Will you give me the canteen if the soldier doesn't want to take it?"

"We'll see," she said.

Tuvia wasn't home from work yet, and Hagar prepared supper. She cut up the tomatoes and the onions, cooked the rice, cleaned the cheese. Yiftach sat at the table and listened to the radio.

Later she gave him his supper and sat opposite him drinking coffee.

"Why aren't you eating with me?" asked Yiftach.

"I'm waiting for Tuvia," she said.

When he finished eating Yiftach went to the window and peered outside.

"I think my dad's back," he said. "I have to go."

"Don't you want a little more ice cream?"

He sat down again, and when she served the ice cream he asked: "Where did you put the canteen?"

"In the cupboard, outside."

He licked the spoon, laid it on the table, said thank you, and went outside.

Hagar switched off the radio, went into the dark bedroom, lay down on the bed and waited.

The electric light from the kitchen fell faintly onto the wardrobe standing next to the wall, opposite the bed. It was quiet in the street, and in the house too. Her tired legs lay heavily on the bed. The quiet and the darkness made it easier for her to breathe. She lay without moving.

Later the street filled with the noise of a motor. She heard gears shifting. The noise came closer to the walls of the house, and then invaded it together with the wind bursting through the window screen.

The noise stopped. The iron gate closed. Her husband's heavy steps climbed the stairs. She didn't have the strength to rise from the bed.

Tuvia didn't come inside. She heard him sitting down on the stairs, taking off his shoes and changing into slippers. She felt tired, she wanted to sleep.

But when he opened the kitchen door she got up.

"You came home late today," she said.

"The work's never done," he said.

"Are you hungry?"

He was unshaven and his hands were black with grease.

"I want to take a shower first," he said.

"Go on then. I'll bring you your clothes."

He went to shower and she switched on the radio, returned to the bedroom and opened the wardrobe. She didn't put the light on in the room. She knew where everything was even in the dark, and she took out a pair of clean trousers, a checked shirt, and underwear. For a moment she looked into the mirror on the wardrobe door. She saw her silhouette against the background of the light wall. The pile of clothes in her arms made her body seem broader, rough and shapeless.

When he emerged from the bathroom the table was already laid.

"Were there any letters?" he asked.

"No."

"What did you do this afternoon?"

"I went for a walk with Yiftach in the Arab village. Simcha's wife's having trouble with the baby."

"I think you need something to do. It's impossible to do nothing but wander around. Without anything."

"I thought about it today too, while we were walking."

She made coffee and said: "Maybe during the long vacation I'll finish my teaching exams. I can be a teacher at the school."

"Do you think you can do it?"

"Why not?"

She cleared the table and stacked the dishes in the sink. The slices of bread on the table had hardened in the heat given off by the kitchen walls. Tuvia went on sitting at the table. He fiddled with the radio knobs. Hagar headed for the bathroom. "Why don't we go out for a bit?" Tuvia called after her. Hagar didn't answer, but when she returned to the kitchen they went out for a walk. It was quiet outside, and pleasant after the heat of the day. They walked as far as Noah Bulkin's place. The house was in darkness, and they heard only the clucking of the hens and the cheeping of their chicks rising from the henhouse.

On their way back they walked down the main street and passed Kasos's cafe. A few elderly people were sitting crowded around a table playing dominoes. Noah Bulkin sat in a corner, drinking beer and reading a newspaper.

When they got home they went straight to bed.

"There's a lot of work now," he said. "I'm tired."

"Where shall we go this summer?" she asked.

"We'll see," he said, "but we'll have to leave it for a month or so. We're snowed under with work. Today we hardly had time for lunch."

A car drove down the road. After it had gone past silence fell again. They lay awake in the dark. A rustle ran through the trees in the yard. Someone seemed to be climbing the steps.

"Did you hear anything?" he asked.

"Nothing," she said.

Again there was a rustle in the trees, and it seemed that the gate creaked. Then all was silent again.

Tuvia fell asleep first. Hagar went on lying awake, with her eyes closed, listening to the sounds of the night.

At midnight she too fell asleep.

6

It was night. Yiftach sat on a jagged stone in the corner of the empty lot where the children always played soccer. The solitary eucalyptus tree standing in the corner of the lot cast a heavy shadow over the stone and over Yiftach. Against the heavy shadow the ground seemed light, and thorn bushes and grass glimmered along its edges.

Little by little the full moon shifted the shadow of the eucalyptus tree. When the children came the stone on which Yiftach was sitting was already in the lighter part of the empty lot.

"Look at him," said Tzemach, "he's the first today."

School was nearly over, the teachers no longer gave homework, and the children felt that the long vacation had begun. In addition to the afternoon games on the lot, they would meet at the eucalyptus tree at night too, after supper, to hide among the bushes, to make bonfires.

"Did your mother let you come out tonight?"

"Can't you see there aren't any lights on in their house? His mother took their baby on the bus."

"His mother," said Tzemach, "could be our grandmother."

Yiftach stood up and kept quiet.

"What do you want of his mother?" said Yoram. "All she did was marry late."

To be exact, at the age of thirty-eight. Until then she had lived in the shack behind Kasos's cafe, cleaned the restaurant once a week, and sometimes cooked. She did the cleaning and laundry for Tzemach's parents too. His father was a clerk in the local council and his mother was too young to occupy herself with such things. For a time Sarah had also worked as a cook in the school kitchen. People had called her Surika.

Sarah would eat her supper in Kasos's cafe, where she was the only regular customer besides Noah Bulkin, all of whose attempts to approach her came to nothing.

"If you can't get anywhere with her, Bulkin," Kasos would say to him, "you'll never get married."

And at night, when she was no longer in the cafe, and the men were tired of playing dominoes or cards, Tabak the grocer would ask Bulkin: "So who does she ever talk to?"

Bulkin would scratch his head, at a loss to reply, and Tabak would continue: "Even in my shop, she hardly says anything. She points to what she wants to buy, and she never checks the bill."

After the war a refugee with a green number on his arm and white hair on his head arrived in the colony. He began working as a janitor at the school, and there, in the kitchen, Surika began to talk to him. His name was Alexander, and they would eat their supper together in the cafe, and talk. He left the little hotel next to the square, and moved into her shack, which during the day was covered by the shade of the pines standing around Kasos's cafe. They stopped going to the cafe every evening for supper, and Tabak ventured to remark that she had begun buying more groceries, "but it's not really right what they're doing, especially at their age, especially in a place like that." This comment was mild compared to his wife's behavior to Alexander that evening. When he came into the grocery store and asked for cheese "like Surika buys," she said to him: "Tell me what you want. If Surika wants goat's cheese let her

39

come for it herself. You're not her husband." And Alexander, in his slow, deep voice answered her: "That's right. But we eat together. . . ."

And then one evening, after Alexander and Surika had eaten at the cafe, they stayed at their table until the men arrived, with Tabak among them. When they began dealing out the dominoes, Surika got up and left. Alexander remained at the table, where two empty cups were standing, with dry breadcrumbs between them. Then he stood up and moved his chair over to join the players, as if it were the most natural thing in the world. He watched the game in silence until Tabak remarked: "Maybe we should find some new game, I'm getting sick and tired of dominoes," and then he asked: "Can you play chess?" and Tabak replied, "Yes."

There were no pieces at Kasos's, and Alexander said, "Just a minute," and went outside. After a few moments he returned from Surika's shack with a folding cardboard chessboard and a tin box containing the kings, the queens, the knights, bishops, rooks and pawns.

When they set out the pieces on the board it turned out that a white pawn was missing. Tabak took a box of matches out of his pocket, broke one of the matches in half, and placed it on the empty square as a pawn.

In the first game Alexander played nervously, like someone excited by an unexpected meeting with an old love, and Tabak, although he kept referring in Yiddish to the fact that it had been a long time since he had last played chess, won.

In the second game, Alexander mentioned the same fact with regard to himself, and Tabak was silent. His head was lowered over the board, and his pale eyes darted over the squares and the black chessmen. He picked his teeth with a used match, and his left foot tapped nervously under the table. Both of them thought slowly, and the game lasted a long time. It was only when Kasos remarked that he couldn't keep the cafe open forever that Tabak said: "Stalemate." They agreed on a draw. Everyone else had already gone home to bed, leaving Noah Bulkin, who didn't know how to play, glued to the table as a mute, solitary witness to the result.

But the true result of the game only became apparent the next morning, when Surika went into the store to buy a loaf of bread. "Your husband's already bought bread," said Tabak.

But Surika and Alexander never got married.

Surika had come to town in reply to an advertisement for a secretary at Peretz's transport company. By the time she arrived the job was already taken, but she stayed on anyway, and since it was winter, she set to work immediately picking fruit. She worked two shifts a day, and at the end of the season she acquired the abandoned shack behind the cafe. When summer came she had no work, and until Kasos, on the basis of an unguarded remark which somehow turned into an obligation, agreed to give her an occasional job cooking and a regular part-time job cleaning the cafe, she spent her time repairing the walls of the shack. Alone she repapered the outside walls with black tar paper, alone she painted the windows, alone she unloaded the truck and carried the table, the small wardrobe, and the new bed linen into the shack.

The shack became the address for housewives who

couldn't cope with the laundry by themselves, or who needed the house cleaned in honor of Sabbath guests. There were the unsatisfied looks of Noah Bulkin which never turned into words. There was the work at the school. And there was Alexander.

About Alexander, apart from his white hair, the gray suit which he always wore without a tie, and his chess games at night, nothing was known. Even though he was the school janitor. His nose was always red and swollen, and his complexion was pale and transparent.

At the school his relationship with the children remained distant. And they, although they called him "Surika's husband," could not hide the hostility which lay behind this apparently natural phrase.

The children's parents too, although they grew accustomed to the fact that they were a steady couple, whose presence had to be occasionally suffered at the cinema, the shops, the public meetings, and the main street of the town on Saturday afternoons, still said to each other: "Let them get married, and then everything will be all right."

Surika and Alexander scraped together the money to buy a house in the street where Hagar and Tuvia Erlich's house now stood, but on the day they were supposed to move in, as suddenly as he had appeared in the town, Alexander disappeared again. As on the previous occasion, this time also nobody helped Surika to move her things into the new house. She put them on the empty lot opposite the house, bought a hard brush from Tabak, and began scrubbing the walls and floors. She moved the furniture in, once more by herself, at night, at the same time as Tabak appeared in the cafe and announced: "We'll have to play dominoes again." For although Alexander had left his chess pieces at the cafe, just as he had left a few pairs of old shoes at Surika's, there was no one apart from Tabak who knew how to move them around the board with any logic at all.

"She's got no luck, that woman," said Kasos, as if to himself, as he brought the players their usual beer.

Surika went on working at the school as if nothing had happened. She did the cooking as usual, and at first, while the pots were cooking on the stove, she swept the playground too, replacing the janitor who had vanished without a word.

When she was sitting in the cafe one evening Tabak winked at Noah Bulkin as if to say: "Go to her, this is your chance." But although Bulkin accompanied Surika home that night, nothing came of it. People began looking at her differently. The disapproving eyes grew more compassionate and the spiteful tongues stopped wagging. Kasos even invited her to a family dinner one Friday night with his wife and sons, a meal that took place in the restaurant kitchen, on a round black table spread with a freshly laundered white cloth.

The winter which washed over the road and the square, the summer which peeled the paint from the walls and opened black cracks in the earth gradually faded Alexander's memory, and Surika went back to being the lonely woman who never spoke. Even though she sometimes appeared in the green dress with the embroidered

43

sleeves that Alexander had bought her for Passover, and gray threads crept into her short hair and wrinkles furrowed her brow, nobody paid any attention to the changes in her.

There was one more episode, but it was short-lived. For one week Surika went out with Tabak's eldest son, who was in his late twenties, several years younger than she was. They went to the movies together on Saturday night, after he had infuriated his parents by having dinner with her at her new house the night before. The Saturday after that, when Surika met Tabak and his wife in the square, Tabak said to her: "What do you want with my son? Leave him alone." Surika thought for a moment, and then she said: "Mr. Tabak, your son is nothing to be proud of." That night she went to the movies alone, and about a month later she began buying groceries at Tabak's shop again.

In the meantime new houses went up in the colony, and new people were seen in the cinema. The eucalyptus grove next to the main road was cut down, and a hospital went up in its place. The construction of the hospital was completed just as the surrounding Arab villages were occupied, and the first wounded were treated there. The school gained a high fence, trees, and a playground. Noah Bulkin built a modern henhouse in his yard.

In the fruit-picking season new truck drivers arrived in town, and Kasos, who knew one of them, Simcha Strauss, made it his business to bring him and Sarah together. One day she had to travel to Haifa, and he arranged for her to go with Simcha. When they returned she climbed out of the driver's cab wearing a new dress, and that same week, on Saturday night, they waltzed together at the party Kasos gave for his son's bar mitzvah.

It was this waltz which gave rise to obscure forebodings in the hearts of the onlookers. Suddenly Simcha reminded them of the white-haired Alexander. The men remembered the night when Kasos had installed the gramophone in the cafe. Besides the chess pieces, Alexander had two records at home. He had loaned them to Kasos for the cafe, and while Tabak shuffled and reshuffled the dominoes, Alexander invited Surika to dance with him between the silent tables. As they danced they drew very close together, and a black domino slipped from Tabak's practiced fingers and fell to the floor.

When there were no more crates left to transport to the harbor it seemed that Simcha Strauss would disappear, go home to his village, and another attempt to rescue Surika from her loneliness would come to nothing. And for two days he did, indeed, disappear; but when he returned it was clear that he had come to stay. The back of his truck was packed with furniture, boxes, iron bars, and a few old cans of kerosene.

The boxes and cans they left in the yard, and the furniture they carted into the house. Even before they had settled on the permanent arrangement of the furniture in the rooms, they held a modest marriage ceremony in the presence of the Kasos and Tabak families. The ceremony took place in the rabbi's house, which was not far from the school, on the road leading to the council house. Since winter was already over, and the kind of summer called spring had arrived, the wedding canopy was erected in the shade of the spreading ficus tree next to the gate. Passers-by stopped for a moment in the street to participate wordlessly in Sarah's great joy and the quiet satisfaction of Kasos, whose cafe was closed for the day in honor of the occasion.

Tabak presented them with two bottles of wine, which they put in the sideboard Simcha had brought on his truck. During the first year of their marriage they both continued their previous ways of life. Sarah, who had given up her job at the school, worked as a fruit-picker, and Simcha went on working as a driver, this time for Peretz's hauling company.

Opposite their house Erlich, the owner of the soda pop factory, built a house for his oldest son, and on Saturdays Simcha put up a toolshed in the yard with the leftover blocks. Although she was pregnant Sarah kept on with the fruit-picking, and when Yiftach was born, exactly a year after the wedding, Simcha sold his truck, and with the money he bought an electrical appliance store in the center of town, where he also maintained a workshop for repairs.

At first the business didn't bring in much money. Nobody trusted Simcha Strauss because, as Tabak said, "How can a truck driver be an electrician?" Nevertheless, Sarah stopped working. She was breast-feeding the baby, and if she had any spare time after doing the housework, she spent it cultivating the garden in front of the house. She planted chrysanthemums all along the veranda and beds of pansies under the window.

Hagar and Tuvia Erlich moved into their new house when Yiftach was three years old. After a few months Hagar stopped attending the teachers' college, and since she finished doing her housework in the morning, and they didn't yet have much of a garden to cultivate, a friendly relationship soon sprang up between herself and her neighbor, Sarah. When Sarah pushed Yiftach down the street in his stroller, and people exchanged knowing looks and exclaimed, "See what a fine son she has," Hagar was unaware of the pitying tone behind the admiring words, and an inexplicable jealousy would stab her heart.

But this faint stab, which stirred in her heart like a weak, trembling chord, did not prevent her from taking care of little Yiftach for three days, when Sarah said to her one evening: "One of my best friends is ill. He's dying, and I have to go to him." The next morning she said good-bye to her husband and left. The neighbors knew nothing of this trip until she returned. In Kasos's cafe the gramophone played old, familiar tunes which touched delicate chords, giving rise to an obscure emotion in the hearts of those present. Tabak was the first to remember that they were Alexander's records. "Him again," he blurted out, addressing himself to Noah Bulkin. Kasos immediately intervened, saying quietly to the players: "That's enough, Mr. Tabak. You may be the owner of a grocery store, but Alexander, the man you used to play chess with, died yesterday in Netanya. When he left us he left his chessmen here in the cafe. And now that he's left this world, he's sent us these records with Sarah. You, Mr. Tabak, would have taken them with you to the grave."

"Don't be such a saint, Kasos," said Tabak. "He made a fool of Sarah when he was here, and now she goes running to him."

"But he's dead, Mr. Tabak, and somebody had to be at his side."

Tabak's hands shook slightly. On the old record the violins squealed, and he tried to place a domino on the table. He stretched his hand out to the upturned dominoes, and then he withdrew it. He changed the domino in his hand for another one, and before adding it to the row, he said: "Yes. I think you're right. Someone had to see him out."

Tabak's wife didn't take in the fact of Alexander's death, and she told Tzemach's mother that Sarah had been away from home for three days, and that she had gone to Alexander. "Is she starting again?" said Tzemach's mother, but Mrs. Tabak did not reply, and went on serving her in silence.

For a few days people whispered behind Sarah's back, and even the kindergarten teacher felt obliged to warn the children not to "say bad things" about Yiftach's mother. Hagar paid no attention to any of this. As if nothing had happened, she went on going for walks with Sarah and her son in the afternoons, in the park, in the street, and on the main road.

But one day Yiftach came home early from kindergarten, crying.

"They talk about me all the time," he said.

Since lunch was ready, his mother served up the hot
soup, the meatballs, and the salad and afterward she
asked him to help her with the laundry. He went to
gather firewood behind the shed, and she sorted out the
clothes in the sink. She arranged the logs and dry twigs in
the stove, under the cauldron, threw on a bit of kerosene,
and handed him the matches.

"Light it," she said.

He was afraid, his fingers trembled, and the match
would not light.

She put her hand on his, and with her help the match
caught fire.

"It's easy," she said, "you see." They threw the burning
match onto the wood, and the fire, which caught quickly,
burst upward, sending a wave of searing heat onto
Yiftach's face.

In the meantime Simcha's electricity shop prospered.
He received orders to install the lighting for bar mitz-
vahs, weddings, graduation ceremonies at the school.
Sarah took care of the chrysanthemums in the garden,
and before Passover, when her husband took another
worker into the shop, she even painted the shutters by
herself.

Yiftach never came home early from kindergarten
again, and when he went to school he did well. Every
evening Sarah checked his homework, and when summer
came she registered him at Zvi Kessler's library, which

was mainly intended for children, but Sarah took books out there too, in order to learn stories to tell to Yiftach when they went for walks.

When Yiftach started the third grade, his little brother was born. They called him Danny, but he didn't react when they spoke to him. His face was blank, and when they passed their hands before his eyes he didn't blink. He cried without making a sound, and no noise woke him. He grew fat, kept his hands stretched out in front of him, but only his body grew. Yiftach read stories about pirates and witches, and his mother traveled to doctors. The truth was that they had already told her in the hospital that it was hopeless, and recommended leaving the baby in a home for retarded children, but Sarah refused, and she took him home. She would take him, too, for walks in the street, covering the white pram, which had belonged to Yiftach when he was a baby, with a fine net to protect him from the mosquitoes, and from the prying eyes.

He never learned to sit, but when he was one year old he learned to crawl. He would crawl in his crib, in his playpen, and sometimes, nobody knew how, he would get out of the playpen and crawl along the walls, scratching the paint with his fingernails.

At first Sarah would follow in his footsteps, repainting the walls in soft pastel shades, with the same perseverance as she went on looking after her flowers. But as the baby's body grew, and as his reactions became more and more incomprehensible, she left the scratches made by his fingernails on the walls, and she stopped taking care of the garden too.

Simcha, who could not bear the sight of the neglected, wilting flowers, would get up early on Saturday mornings and do his best to keep the yard in shape. But the baby's condition depressed him too.

"It's a pity I sold the Volvo," he said one morning, and he stopped getting up to water the flowers. He went on working in the shop from morning to night, and during the holidays he would sometimes take Yiftach with him. The pansies all died long ago, and the chrysanthemums grew wild, stopped flowering and spread to the fence, mingling with the thorns and weeds which shot up between the tender seedlings of grass, seedlings which never joined up into a lawn, and without a hand to guide them the wild things overran the yard, the fence, and the walls.

Yiftach would sit in the kitchen and do his homework. He would go to the grocer's and watch the food cooking on the stove. When he walked down the street with his hair combed and his shoulders stooped, a basket full of groceries in his hand, Tzemach's mother would say: "Just look at that little man." And after a short pause, she would repeat a remark which from time to time escaped the lips of others too: "When they dished out good luck that woman was at the end of the line."

Sarah and Simcha stopped going to the cinema, but on the rare occasions when they did go out, Yiftach would lie awake next to his little brother's bed until they came home. He would read the picture books he took out of

Zvi Kessler's library, and if he hadn't fallen asleep by the time all the pages were turned, he would begin again from the beginning.

Sarah stopped talking again. She restricted herself to essential words, and in Tabak's grocery store she would point to the things she wanted to buy, and never check the bill.

7

After supper at Hagar Erlich's Yiftach did not go home. He reached the gate, and when he saw that his house was dark, he went to the lot. There was nobody there yet. He sat on the stone and waited. He saw Tuvia's jeep sending long beams into the street, and then he saw the light go on in the bathroom.

Yiftach watched the lights going on and off in Hagar and Tuvia's house until they went out altogether, and then he stood up and approached the fence surrounding the dark house. Although Hagar had forgotten to shut the front gate, and the side gate through which Tuvia had driven the jeep was unlocked too, he decided to go in through the fence. He lifted the branches of the vine clinging to the barbed wire, and, like a fox, crawled under the bottom strand into the yard.

The heat of the day was still heavy among the fruit trees, and when he passed under the boughs of the tangerine a cloud of mosquitoes moved with him and his skin itched. In the shelter of the trees he paused. Between them and the veranda lay a stretch of open ground, with the clear light of the full moon shining on it. Voices echoed in the street. It seemed to him that Tuvia and Hagar were returning, or maybe someone was coming to visit them. But the moon sailing through the sky moved away, a shadow fell over the stretch of open ground, and Yiftach ran to the veranda and stopped next to the steps. All around him it was quiet. The howling of the jackals had not yet begun in the orange grove. He shrank into the corner between the steps and the wall.

After a while he took off his sandals, and holding them in his hand he climbed the steps to the veranda. He went up to the tall, narrow cupboard built into the corner of the wall, looked around him, and tried to open the door. The door was locked. His feet were cold. He went down the steps and stretched his hand up to the windowsill. His hand touched the cold marble, but his fingers did not reach the place under the can where he knew the keys were kept.

With his hand raised he jumped up. The first time he didn't even touch the can. The second time he knocked it over. The can fell to the ground, hit a pail, and vanished in the darkness. It seemed to him that the keys had fallen too. He bent down, put his sandals on the ground, and began groping in the sand. His fingers encountered a few sharp stones, dry leaves and bits of wood. But no keys. There was a rustle in the trees. A jackal or cat raced past. He stood still.

The animal came up against the fence, and in its struggle to break out, it shook the dry branches which made a whistling, whispering sound.

He turned the pail over and climbed onto it. Now he reached the window sill easily. After a brief, groping search, his fingers encountered the key ring. There were only two keys on it – one, long and thick, the key to the house, and the second, shorter one, the key to the veranda cupboard.

Leaving his sandals next to the overturned pail he climbed the cold veranda steps again. Everything was silent, and when he pushed the key into the keyhole it made a faint noise which rooted him to the spot. He pressed against the door and slowly turned the key. The long, narrow door opened. The veranda was dark, and inside the cupboard, which was set deep into the wall, he at first couldn't see anything at all. But then he managed to make out a few shelves at the bottom. He knelt down and began to rummage. He felt smooth cans of shoe polish, rough brushes, newspapers, a few baskets, and a cardboard box full of clothespins. He raised his hands to the second shelf. Two empty metal pots sent a cold current through the tips of his fingers. His hands tangled with slack coils of rope and string.

His knees hurt. He stood up and leaned against the wall. Then he bent down again, supporting himself with one hand on the wall, while the other searched. The third shelf was full of newspapers, and among them, in the corner, his fingers encountered the thin chain which attached the cork to the canteen.

When he pulled it toward him, a few newspapers were dislodged and fell onto the floor. He picked them up, put them back on the shelf, closed the door and locked it. Then he climbed down the steps and returned to the up-ended pail. He climbed onto it and put the keys back on the windowsill. While he was putting on his sandals he suddenly remembered that he had forgotten to replace the can which had covered the keys. He found it easily, lying on the sand between two dry, thorny branches. He put it on the windowsill, on top of the keys, turned the pail over, and got ready to leave.

He intended going out by the big side gate through which Tuvia always drove the jeep into the yard. But even when he was standing in the shadow of the jeep the aluminum of the uncovered canteen glittered in his hand, and he turned on his heel and retraced his steps. This time he avoided going past the veranda and went straight into the trees. He listened to the noise of his footsteps and his body brushing against the branches, and made for the fence. Without trying to locate the exact spot where he had entered the yard, he thrust the supports propping up the vines aside, threw the canteen through the fence, and crawled after it. The barbed wire caught his shirt, and when he pulled it free, it tore.

His father had not yet come home, and Yiftach went into the shed and filled the canteen with water. He took a few sips, and filled it up again. There was a stifling smell in the shed, and he washed his face, dried it on his shirt and went outside. When he had gone a few paces in the dew-drenched grass, he heard muffled footsteps in the road. His father opened the gate and Yiftach retreated, walked around the shed, and hid behind it, among the piles of old crates and planks which he used to feed the fire under the boiling laundry.

He listened attentively to his father's footsteps. He heard him stop outside the door and rummage in his tool bag for the key. A weak beam of light flooded the yard as the door creaked open. From the shadows in which he was hiding the yard looked pale, like the night.

In the kitchen and hall the lights were already on, but he could not see his father's silhouette. He walked slowly along the clotheslines, circled the house, and stole out the gate into the street.

The lights of a tractor driving past dazzled him. He pushed the canteen inside his torn shirt. Under the shirt his skin was bare, and a shiver of cold ran down his belly. But then the warmth of his body overcame the chill of the aluminum and apart from its heavy jolting he hardly felt the canteen. He made for the spreading shadow of the eucalyptus tree. He sat down on the stone in the corner of the lot, put the canteen behind it, and waited for the children.

There were six of them, including him. And when they arrived, they all headed for the school. Between the school and the cemetery was a plowed field, with the remains of an old army training ground still standing between its furrows. There were tall poles, bars for balancing, a framed net, and rope ladders. The furrows were deep and dry. Occasionally they tripped on clods of earth. The race to the rope ladder was won by Tzemach, who was the oldest. The rest of them stumbled behind him, between the furrows, but Yiftach didn't come last.

The canteen was hidden under his shirt again, but nobody had yet noticed his bulging stomach. As he ran his shirttails escaped from his trousers, but he caught the canteen before it fell. When he reached the rope ladder, the canteen was safely tucked into his shirt again.

Tzemach held onto the rope ladder with both hands and panted for breath. When the last boy arrived, Tzemach began to climb. The ropes swayed, and since they were not clearly visible, Tzemach seemed to be floating in the air. He climbed down and they went up after him. Yiftach remained standing to one side.

He opened the canteen and began to drink from it.

"Why don't you go up?" asked Tzemach.

"I'm thirsty," said Yiftach and took a sip of water.

"What have you got there?" asked Yoram.

"A canteen," said Yiftach, "can't you see?"

"His mother must have given it to him. A toy canteen, made of rubber."

"I got it for myself," said Yiftach. "It's tin. A soldier's canteen."

"You've got a big imagination," Tzemach sneered.

"You can touch it if you don't believe me."

Tzemach stayed where he was. But Yoram said: "Give us a sip."

"In a minute." Yiftach took another sip and closed the canteen. Then he hooked his little finger round the chain attached to the cork, and offered the canteen to Yoram.

"It's heavy," said Yoram.

"I've already drunk half of it," said Yiftach, "so imagine how much it weighs when it's full."

Yoram lifted the canteen to his lips to drink. But Tzemach took a step toward him and pushed the canteen, which fell to the ground. The water spilled out and soaked into the earth.

Yiftach went up to it and picked it up. It was smeared with mud. He cleaned it with his shirt and then he held it by the cork. The canteen hung next to his thigh.

"Look at him," said Yoram. "He's envious."

"Go home to your mommy," said Tzemach. "She has to check your homework."

Yiftach did not reply. He went up to the rope ladder, sat on the second rung, and swung to and fro.

"What do you want of him?" asked Yoram.

"You shut your mouth. Sucking up to everybody. It's not a soldiers' canteen."

"It is a soldiers' canteen," said Yiftach. "A certain soldier's." He got off the ladder. "Tomorrow I'm going to give it back to him. I've got a date to meet him."

Tzemach laughed. He moved toward Yiftach and a fight seemed about to break out. Yiftach too took a step forward. Tzemach bent down and picked up a small clod of earth.

"No stones," someone shouted.

But Tzemach didn't have time to hear the shout. Yiftach sprang on him, hit him with his fists, and ran away, far into the plowed field.

They ran after him. He could hear their cries and stumbles. He too tripped several times, but he didn't stop running. His feet drew him in the direction of the cemetery. But when he reached the gravedigger's hut he was brought up short by fear, and he began retracing his steps. Their voices were close. He lay down on the field, dug himself in between two ridges of earth, and curled into a ball.

They were all around him, scattered over the ground, calling loudly to each other. Yiftach shrank, he lay still and tried not to breathe.

"He must have gone into the cemetery," someone called.

"Who? That coward?" said Tzemach.

They searched, and he lay on the ground, shrinking and dirty. From his hiding place he could see their shadows moving. The moon made them long and tall. He himself had no shadow. It was already late and he had to go home. But the children went on roaming around the field.

When they were tired of searching, Tzemach said: "Don't worry. He'll have to go back to his mother. We'll catch him tomorrow."

They returned to the rope ladder, and after a while moved on to the school playground, walking in a close group.

Yiftach followed them. When he heard them leaving the playground and saw their figures in the light shining over the gate, he went into the grounds and headed for the taps. He cleaned the canteen, washed his face and drank water.

He took a roundabout way home. In most of the

houses the lights were already off, and the streets were deserted. He walked slowly along the fences lining the road. There was a pile of gravel outside their house. He climbed it and saw his father's head, bent over a newspaper, through the lighted window. His mother was not yet back.

There was a light on in Hagar and Tuvia Erlich's house. The lot was empty, with only the moon sailing over it. He ran to the shade of the eucalyptus, sat down on the stone, and looked at Hagar's house. He was waiting for the light to go off.

But before it did, he saw his mother passing underneath the streetlights. She was carrying his baby brother in her arms. She opened the gate and went into the house.

He waited a few minutes longer and suddenly he felt terribly thirsty. Although the canteen was empty, he raised it to his lips, hoping that a few drops would fall into his mouth. He licked his lips and as he put the canteen back into his shirt, the light went off in Hagar's house. He stood up and headed for the fence. Again he crawled under it and continued crawling on all fours between the trees. When he drew close to the bedroom window he heard them talking. He took off his sandals and approached the veranda with quiet steps.

"I haven't got a key," he suddenly said to himself. But he climbed the steps nevertheless and went up to the cupboard door. He bumped into Tuvia's work boots, which were standing on top of the balustrade, and the scraping of the nails on the stone made him cling to the wall. Tuvia and Hagar stopped talking. Yiftach stood quite still.

When he thought that they had fallen asleep he tiptoed up to the cupboard. The door was locked. A cold sweat bathed his forehead and the fingers of his hands holding his sandals. Next to the cupboard was an empty wicker basket. He lifted the paper lining the bottom of the basket, laid the canteen in the basket, and covered it with the paper. His eyes grew accustomed to the darkness, so that he was able to distinguish various objects on the veranda. A little bench, a crate of plums, a shovel. And then, with a swift, sharp movement, he bent down and took the canteen out of the basket. He tucked it into his shirt and climbed down the veranda steps. Next to the jeep he stopped to put on his sandals, and then he went home. He hid the canteen behind the shed, under an overturned box.

Before going inside he knocked on the door.

"Where have you been?" asked his mother.

"At Hagar's."

"Until now?"

"Yes. I saw you weren't back yet."

"But I was back," said his father.

"And how did you get so dirty?" asked his mother, staring at his torn shirt.

"I played with the kids in the afternoon."

She cut him a slice of cake and made him a cup of tea. When he came back clean from the shower, she asked: "Have you done your homework?"

"She's stopped giving us any. The holidays start next week."

"But you should go over your lessons. Even if I haven't got the time to sit with you."

She turned to his father. "I'm taking the baby to the hospital again tomorrow morning. Maybe they'll keep him there. I don't know. Something has to be done."

Yiftach went to bed. Sarah went into the kitchen, prepared a salad for breakfast, and put it in the refrigerator. The next morning he woke early. Sarah took care of the baby, Simcha sliced the bread, and Yiftach fried the omelets.

"What time does school finish?" asked his father.

"Twelve o'clock."

"Come to the shop. We'll go and have lunch together." He stroked Yiftach's head. "And then we'll go and get our hair cut."

"Okay," said Yiftach. But when he went out of the door he didn't turn toward the gate. He went around to the back of the shed, put the canteen into his satchel, and then crossed the street to Hagar Erlich's house. Moving cautiously, he approached the veranda and climbed the steps. The cupboard door was open. The boot brush and can of polish were standing on the balustrade. The can was open. He pushed the canteen into the cupboard and was covering it with newspapers when the kitchen door opened and Hagar Erlich came out onto the veranda.

"Yiftach," she exclaimed, "what are you doing here?"

"My mother had to go out today too," he said, "and

she asked if you could take me for a walk this afternoon."

8

In the morning, Hagar boiled up a pot of Turkish coffee and put it in the refrigerator. And at midday, after she had finished cooking, she packed the meal she had prepared for her husband into the wicker basket and took the bus to the garage.

Tuvia was sitting on the fender of a car whose engine had been taken apart. His blue overalls were covered with grease stains. Yoel was wearing khaki, and his overalls were lying next to him. They were talking.

"See you later," said Yoel, picked up his overalls, and turned to go.

He went over to the office, threw the overalls onto a rough black tire lying next to the door, and when he turned his head he saw Hagar.

"What are you doing here?" he asked.

"Nothing," she said. "I came to see you and Tuvia." She was wearing a green skirt scattered with red flowers, and a thin, yellow sleeveless blouse. The wicker basket in her hand brushed her white knees.

Tuvia overheard their conversation. He got off the fender, put the wrench in his hand on the concrete floor of the garage, and walked over to his wife. He kissed her without touching her with his hands.

"My hands are dirty," he said.

He took the wicker basket from her, and when they were on their way to the office, he asked: "What made you decide to come?"

"I thought that if we ate here, you would have time to rest, and you wouldn't have to waste time on the drive."

They went into the office. Tuvia put the basket down on a chair and went over to the sink, and Hagar cleared away the account books scattered over the surface of the table.

It was cool inside the office, which was a long room with plastered but unpainted walls. On the outside the gray blocks were naked and exposed. For some reason, the cool air in the room made Hagar feel tired, and she sat down next to the table.

"It's actually chilly in here," she said, "but suddenly I feel as if I haven't got any strength."

Tuvia's sleeves were rolled up, his arms and hands full of soap. He washed off the soap and dried himself on the threadbare towel hanging on the window over the sink.

"In a month's time," he said, "we can go for a holiday." And turning to face her, he added: "This year we'll go first."

She spread a cloth over the table, took the plates and cutlery out of the basket and set them on it. Then she opened the cupboard, got out the electric kettle and filled it with water. When Tuvia sat down at the table she took a bottle of red wine out of the basket.

"I'm glad you came," he said. "Lately we seem to have drifted a little apart."

"Yes. I need something to do. I've got too much spare time."

"Maybe you should write home and ask them to send your books."

"Do you think I can do it?"

"If you work."

They ate spicy meatballs and drank wine. Every now and then they heard the roar of a car speeding past on the highway. Because of the chilly air in the room it seemed as if a breeze was blowing outside. But the trees outside the window were motionless.

"Yiftach's going to have lunch at our house," she said as they drank their coffee. "His mother's taken the baby to the hospital again."

Tuvia said nothing. He gripped the handle of his cup and stared at the black coffee.

"Is anything wrong?" she asked.

"There's nothing wrong with Yiftach, he's fine. But Sarah, you know . . . and the baby's not normal. . . ."

"What about Sarah?"

"You're not from here. I still remember her wrapping oranges in the citrus grove. And living alone in that shack. Why haven't you got any other friends?"

"You don't need to worry about me and my friends. I can take care of myself. What have you got against Sarah?"

His eyes remained fixed on the cup of coffee. "Have you seen the way everyone looks at her?" he said.

Hagar stood up and opened the window, leaned on the cool sill and looked outside. Next to the police station she saw Yoel's jeep coming back. She returned to the table, packed the dishes in the basket, and walked out of the room, leaving her unfinished coffee on the table.

"Do you want me to drive you home?" Tuvia called after her.

"No need," she said. "I'll take the bus."

At home she stacked the dishes in the sink, and then she laid the table with a single place. For Yiftach. When he didn't come, she washed the dishes, and after she had finished she heard a knock at the door. Yiftach walked in, his satchel on his back. His hair was cut, and there were bits of hair on his shirt.

"You finished school so late?" She went up to him and took the satchel off his back. "Your lunch is ready."

"I already ate, with my dad," he said.

"Really? Where?"

"At Kasos's."

"You don't get a decent meal at Kasos's. Why don't you eat what I made for you too? It isn't much. I see you had time for a haircut too."

"Yes. My dad took me. Leibowitz was still open and there wasn't anybody before us."

Yiftach ate a meatball and after that he and Hagar both had stewed fruit. Throughout the meal he kept looking at Hagar as if there was something he wanted to tell her. Hagar noticed, but she didn't say anything.

66

The shutters were closed and the house was in semi-darkness, with a light burning in the kitchen.

"You can take your sandals off and go barefoot if you like," said Hagar.

He sat huddled on the chair, his teaspoon in the empty dish.

She patted his shirt and brushed off the hairs sticking to it.

"Do you want to wash?" She cleared the dishes off the table. "Take a shower, and then you can have a rest."

"I want to put my satchel away at home," he said. "I can wash there."

"You can leave your satchel here," she said. She put on her apron and turned on the tap over the sink. "Go and take a shower, you'll feel better. We'll have a little rest, and later in the afternoon we'll go for a walk in the Arab village again."

Yiftach did not reply.

"If we meet the soldier we'll return the canteen." The irritating splashing of the water muffled her words, but he distinctly heard her say: "If he doesn't want to take it back, I'll let you keep it."

His hands gripped the edge of the table, his fingers squeezing hard. He was afraid to look at her. His eyes were fixed on the table. It seemed to him that his new haircut changed the shape of his face, and he no longer looked like himself.

"I don't need the canteen," he said quickly.

"Why?" she asked, turning to look at him. A lock of hair fell over her eyes. She brushed the hair off her face with her arm. Her hands were covered with a layer of foam.

In the end he took a shower at her house.

A strange smell of shaving soap and cosmetics pervaded the shower. There were two colored towels hanging next to the mirror. Among the bottles of perfume and jars of cream on the shelf, he noticed a rusty razor blade. He looked at himself in the mirror. There were wisps of hair plastered to his forehead, but the part was straight as a ruler. He rumpled his hair with his fingers and got into the shower.

Hagar spread two sheets and a blanket on the living room floor, and Yiftach took off his shirt and sandals, and lay down with the upper half of his torso naked. The shutters were closed and the room was dark.

Yiftach couldn't fall asleep. He tossed and turned for a while and then he got up, turned on the light in the room, and went over to the low bookcase standing next to the window. As he was looking for a book he came across a photograph album. He paged through it and saw Hagar and Tuvia in their youth. He saw their house. On one of the pages he saw his own family, when he was still a baby without any hair. In the picture his mother was wearing an apron, and his father was carrying the bag in which he took his sandwiches to work. His little brother was not yet born. The picture had been taken in the afternoon. His parents' shadows fell to the east of the dirt road. He himself left no mark on the sand.

When he woke up Hagar was already in the kitchen. He washed his face and sat down in his favorite chair.

Hagar went out to the veranda, opened the cupboard, and took out the canteen. She washed it in the sink, and then she opened the refrigerator and filled it with the cold coffee which she had prepared in the morning. The coffee left over in the jar she poured into two cups, adding whipped cream to Yiftach's cup.

"We'll give him a surprise," she said.

"The soldier?"

"Yes. He's not used to having coffee in his canteen. Especially iced coffee."

"How do you know that he'll be there?"

Hagar hesitated for a moment. She sipped her coffee, and then she said: "He'll be there. He's been coming every day for several days now."

Yiftach licked the whipped cream and looked at the canteen standing at the end of the table. It was clean, there wasn't a trace of mud on it.

"The canteen'll get hot," he said.

"I didn't think of that," said Hagar. She wrapped the canteen in a wet cloth and gave it to Yiftach.

"I want you to give it to him," she said.

"I don't need it," said Yiftach, and put it down on the table.

"But yesterday you asked me for it, didn't you?"

They left by the big iron gate through which Tuvia always drove the jeep into the yard. Yiftach didn't speak. Hagar asked him questions, and he responded by jerking his head or mumbling unintelligibly. She held her knitting bag, and he carried the canteen wrapped in the damp, yellow dishcloth. At the end of the road Yiftach picked up a dry branch and trailed it along the wire fence. It made a rhythmic, creaking noise. Hagar didn't say anything.

Instead of walking over the field they took a path leading through the citrus grove. The path was shady, but suddenly mosquitoes appeared, flying into their hair, darting against their foreheads. Yiftach held the canteen loosely. He dragged the dry branch behind him, making a dark groove in the sand. When the path emerged into a patch of sunlight, they blinked, and Yiftach dropped the canteen.

The damp, yellow cloth wrapped around the canteen was muddied by the sand. Hagar put her knitting bag down on the ground, and rubbed the cloth with her hand. Instead of getting the mud off, however, she only succeeded in rubbing it deeper in.

"What's the matter with you?" she asked.

"Nothing," he said.

"Is that why you finally agreed to take the canteen?" The lines on her forehead came together, her face fell. "Look what you've done!"

He was silent.

Hagar unwrapped the cloth from the canteen. She put the canteen into her knitting bag, and held the cloth in her hand.

"Why don't we go into Noah Bulkin's and wash the cloth off?" said Yiftach suddenly. "We go right past his place."

"Where did you get that idea from?"

"I met him today at Leibowitz's barbershop, and he

told me I could come and see him if I felt like it."

Bulkin was not at home. Only the chickens cackled in the henhouse, and the sacks of feed spread a dry warmth. They went into the yard and made for the big tap standing at the entrance to the house. A pair of clean, wet, black rubber boots stood next to it. Yiftach ran up to the tap and drank. When he had finished Hagar washed the cloth, and then she too drank from the tap. She took the canteen out of her bag and wrapped it up again. She looked around the yard for a piece of string. Not finding any, she tore a length of wool from the ball in her knitting bag, and tied the cloth to the canteen with it. The canteen looked like a potbellied water jar, and Yiftach said: "Give it to me, I want to carry it now."

"Careful," said Hagar. Yiftach was standing next to a big can of coagulated glue. Posters with black letters staring from them lay scattered around the can.

"What's this?" Yiftach picked up the rough brush and stuck it into the glue.

"At night he sticks up all kinds of posters on the walls."

"What for?"

"Never mind."

Again they entered the shade between the trees. In the distance a thin spiral of smoke rose into the sky.

"Look," said Hagar. "They're there."

"Who?"

"The soldiers."

"Is he there too?" asked Yiftach.

A stone-paved alley led them to the village. There were

dry cacti withering at its sides. The walls behind the cactus bushes hid ruined houses, piles of rubble. At the bend in the road stood an undamaged house. They went inside, and climbed a staircase to the flat roof.

The soldiers were divided into two groups. One group was sitting on the ground, in the shade of a ruined wall. There was a fire burning between two large stones, which supported long, thin iron spits upon which stood some blackened tin cans. Three soldiers bustled around the fire, feeding the flames with twigs and watching the cans to see that they didn't fall over. One soldier was eating from a can with a spoon. When he had completed his share he passed the can and the spoon to his neighbor.

The second group of soldiers was training. They hid behind a cactus hedge and crept toward an isolated building at the edge of the village. When they reached a hillock covered with thorns at a short distance from the building, they stopped. Two soldiers armed with machine guns dropped to the ground and lay on the slope of the hillock, aiming their guns at the door and windows of the building. The rest of the soldiers went on creeping along the cactus hedge and advanced in a slight flanking movement toward the house. Then they stopped for a moment, and suddenly charged to the entrance and flattened themselves against the wall. The first in the line threw a stone into the room, and after a short pause they all burst into the building and disappeared into the darkness.

From the cooking fire next to the wall smoke spiraled into the sky.

The three men tending the fire were replaced by three others.

After charging the house the soldiers emerged again and returned to the stone fence. They lined up in a row, raised their guns, and inserted the magazines. Then they knelt down. The commander, who was standing, spoke to the kneeling men.

"Are they going to shoot?" Yiftach asked Hagar.

They sat on the flat roof. The full sun was far in the west, close to the invisible sea. A cool wind blew over the roof, brushing their faces. Hagar took the scarf off her head.

"Yes. But don't be afraid. They're not live bullets."

"What are they?"

"Wooden bullets."

"Are you sure?"

The soldiers rose, holding their guns with both hands, and advanced along the cactus hedge.

After a few steps they stopped. All their faces were turned to the roof on which Hagar and Yiftach were sitting. The commander waved his hand, but Hagar and Yiftach did not move from their places. Then one of the soldiers left the row and made his way toward them. He passed between the ruins, disappearing and reappearing alternately. Hagar and Yiftach came down from the roof, emerged from the house, and went to meet the soldier. Next to a blocked well in the middle of a bare, spacious courtyard they met him.

"Hi," said the soldier.

"Hi," said Hagar.

"I've already seen you once before," said the soldier, "but you're not allowed to be here now. Didn't you see the red flags?"

"It was you we walked to the truck with, right?" said Yiftach.

"Yes. But you have to leave now. This is a firing zone and people are shooting here."

"Okay, we're going," said Hagar.

"What about the canteen?" asked Yiftach.

"We'll give it back to him another time."

"Did you bring the canteen?" asked the soldier.

Hagar put her hand out to Yiftach.

"You don't have to leave. You can go back inside the house. Stay there until the firing stops. But don't go up to the roof."

The soldier disappeared between the houses and Hagar and Yiftach went inside. When her eyes got used to the dark, Hagar saw colored tiles in a circle of squares around a white stone in the middle of the room. The floor was dirty.

They sat down on a step, Hagar hugging her knees with her arms while Yiftach stretched his legs out in front of him.

"Have you got the canteen?" asked Yiftach.

"Yes," said Hagar.

"Why didn't you give it to him?"

"We'll give it to him afterward."

"But maybe he won't be the last in line today."

"I got a good look at him," said Hagar. "He'll be the last."

"Listen," said Yiftach. "I want to tell you something. . . ."

He didn't finish the sentence. The firing began. They both fell silent.

When the firing stopped, they heard the clatter of running boots. Yiftach stood up and began climbing the steps. "Wait a bit longer," said Hagar. But Yiftach went on climbing. "Come here," she called. "You said you wanted to tell me something." But Yiftach was already at the top of the stairs. She climbed up after him, and after ascending a few steps she heard a single shot. She stopped, hugged the wall, called Yiftach's name, and started running up the stairs.

The soldiers who had conquered the building came out again, jumping through the windows and the doors. They formed a row and headed for the fire burning under the improvised grill. The soldiers who had been sitting along the wall and eating from the cans strapped on their packs, picked up the weapons which had been propped up against the wall, and moved off. They walked over to the end of the cactus hedge. The flames had all died down, but the wood was still burning, giving off heat and smoke and the glow of shining red embers. Nobody went up to feed the fire. Hagar climbed onto the roof.

Yiftach was sitting on the edge, swinging his legs to and fro in the air, hitting the wall with his feet. He didn't notice Hagar standing behind him, her skin stretched tight over her face, her arms hanging at the sides of her body.

"Didn't you hear the shot?"

Yiftach didn't turn his head.

"Come on," she said. "They haven't finished shooting yet."

"But they're not shooting in this direction, and I want to see them."

"It's dangerous," she said. She grabbed hold of his shirt collar and tugged it. He stood up and followed her, hanging his head.

"You gave me a fright," she said, after they had seated themselves on the step again.

The shooting began again. It went on for a few minutes and then stopped.

"We can go now," said Yiftach.

"We'd better wait a bit longer," said Hagar.

She looked at the window. There was a faint buzzing in her ears. "Was there something you wanted to tell me?"

Yiftach's head was resting on his knees.

"No," he said. "I was just humming."

Rough steps thudded on the stones, and the soldier's head appeared at the window. "We've finished," he said. "You can come out now." He was wearing a steel helmet, and they could see the straps of his backpack on his shoulders. In the shade cast by the helmet his sweat glistened.

They went outside. The soldier remained standing next to the window.

"Is the truck waiting for you?" asked Yiftach. The soldiers were heading for the citrus grove again.

"Yes," said the soldier.

"Why aren't you going with them?" asked Hagar.

"I wanted to tell you that you can come out and walk around again. We're finished."

The three of them walked over to the dying fire. When they reached it the soldier kicked up the ground and covered it with sand. Gray streaks ran down the leather of his boots, which had been rubbed with black boot-polish that morning.

"We've brought something for you," said Hagar.

The soldier looked at her.

"Don't you remember what we talked about yesterday?" she asked.

"But I told you, it's not my canteen."

"It is yours," said Hagar and she reached into her bag and took out the canteen wrapped in the yellow cloth. "Here," she said. "Have a drink."

"A drink is something else," he said. He opened the canteen and took a sip.

"It's coffee!"

There were black drops on his lips. He smiled. The steel helmet was lying on the ground. His gun was propped against the wall. His hair was plastered to his scalp, and streaks of dried, brown sweat ran down his face. His lips were broad and cracked, his cheeks were covered with stubble. His cheekbones were high and bronzed.

He held the canteen in his hand. "The coffee is cold," he said.

Hagar and Yiftach were silent.

The setting sun cast red and gray colors over the

village. The dry grass, because of the shade falling on it, and because of the weak rays of the sun caressing it, looked brighter, green and alive.

A light breeze began to caress the walls of the abandoned houses, and Hagar took the scarf out of her knitting bag and tied it round her head. The blue scarf bared her face and drew a faint shadowy line around her forehead and her pink cheeks. Her lips were pale, her green eyes fixed on the ground.

Without thinking she held out her hand to Yiftach. They held hands as the soldier strapped on his pack and hoisted his gun to his shoulder, holding the canteen in his hand. He began walking away.

He left the path which was lit up by the sun. They were still standing in the shade next to the wall, opposite the two stones on which the soldiers had supported their cooking grid.

He emerged from the patch of sunlight and entered the shade of a low palm with a rough trunk, where he stopped and turned to face Hagar and Yiftach.

"I forgot to thank you," he said. "That was a great idea."

They walked toward him, holding hands. The tail of Hagar's scarf waved in the wind as they joined him next to the palm tree. Wordlessly the soldier handed the canteen to Yiftach. They left the village, crossed the stone wall, and went into the field. At the other end of the field they saw the last soldiers going into the orange grove.

At first they walked side by side, but the thorns got in their way, and so they stepped back onto the narrow path and walked one behind the other. The soldier, Yiftach, and Hagar. The field was exposed to the sun, now balanced on the points of the roofs, and the soldier's face glistened with sweat again. The path broadened, and Hagar walked next to Yiftach.

"Will you be here tomorrow?" asked Yiftach.

"Tomorrow?!" said the soldier. "Tomorrow's Friday, and the next day's Saturday."

"And what will you do?"

Without waiting for an answer, Yiftach held the canteen out to the soldier. "Take it," he said. "It's yours."

"Never mind," said the soldier. "You can keep it."

There was a silence again, but then the soldier, as if recalling Yiftach's question, said: "Tomorrow we clean the weapons and get organized. On Saturday morning we stay in the camp and rest, but in the afternoon we get leave till midnight."

"Will you go home?" asked Hagar.

"No. I live in Haifa. I'll go to Tel Aviv."

"Are you giving me the canteen for a present?" asked Yiftach.

The soldier patted Yiftach on the back. "Yes," he said.

"What will you do in Tel Aviv?" asked Hagar. They were now on the edge of the orange grove.

"What does anyone do in Tel Aviv? Hang around Mograbi. On the promenade."

Yiftach held the canteen in both hands. His eyes were fixed on the yellow dishcloth in which it was wrapped. The soldier took his gun off his shoulder and leaned on it. Hagar tightened the knot of her scarf, and looked at the soldier's brown face. His face was calm, his eyes looked at her without moving. Behind him were the fruitless trees.

"Is he your son?" asked the soldier.

"No," she said quietly.

At the end of the field, in the distance, they saw a small, square van. Noah Bulkin and his Arab worker, Hilmi, were moving around next to it. They approached a low pile of sacks.

The soldier held out his hand to Hagar. They shook hands, said good-bye, and parted. Yiftach and Hagar watched the green and gray uniform disappearing into the trees. In the hollows, between the dry leaves, little purple flowers bloomed.

After that they walked away. The field was empty except for Bulkin and Hilmi loading the sacks onto the back of the van in the distance.

Yiftach and Hagar walked toward them, but they had already finished loading the van. Hilmi closed the tailgate, and joined Bulkin in the cab.

"What's this?" said Yiftach. "Has Bulkin got a van?"

The van drove up to them, and as it came close they could see the two men behind the dusty window. The wheels crushed the grass, broke the thorns and trampled them into the ground.

Bulkin stuck his head out of the window and said "Hello." He wasn't wearing a shirt, and Yiftach saw his broad, hairy shoulders, and the straps of his gray undershirt.

"Since when have you had a van?" he asked.

"Since I got my hair cut today at Leibowitz's," said Bulkin. "You should know all about it. I want to buy a horse. And in order to bring it here I need a van. It's simple."

"Are you buying a horse?" asked Yiftach.

"Yes, next week."

"Where?"

"In the market."

"The market? What market?"

"The horse market. In Acre. You should know. And that's why I bought the van too, in Tuvia's garage." He laughed, and looked at Hagar.

"Congratulations," she said.

"Congratulations to you too," he said. "You'll be able to buy a few more dresses. It's Tuvia's father's Morris. At last it's left the family."

"Do you want a ride?" he asked.

"No," said Hagar.

"Will you take me to the market?" asked Yiftach.

"Of course," said Bulkin.

The Arab sat in the corner of the cab, leaning on the door. He said nothing. The van moved off.

They crossed the field and went up to the road. Cars and carts passed them. Then a dirt road intersected with the highway and they turned into it. It was the road that led to the cemetery, the plowed field, and the school.

"Are you glad you got the canteen?"

Yiftach didn't answer, but every now and then he

grasped the canteen in both hands and held it to his face.

"Give it to me," said Hagar. "I'll sew you a cover for it. From the yellow dishcloth."

To their left was the cemetery, deserted. There was a light on in the gravedigger's hut. The deep furrows in the plowed field were smooth, and where an accidental sunbeam hit them they shone. Yiftach looked at the furrows and bit his lips. He bowed his head and stopped walking.

"Let's go back," he said.

He walked next to her, kicking stones, running ahead and coming back to her. Only when they reached the street where they lived did he seem to calm down.

"Will you give me the canteen, then, so I can sew you a cover for it?"

"You see," he said, "there's a light on in my house." Evening had already invaded the street, and the streetlights were on, even though it was still possible to see without them.

"You know," he said, "there's something I want to tell you. I've been wanting to tell you all day."

He gave her the canteen, and when she put it into her knitting bag, she said: "Tell me then. . . ."

But Yiftach said again: "There's a light on in my house," and began running down the street to his house.

He went into the yard, and the lamp above the front door went on.

The street was deserted. Only the streetlights, without which she still would have been able to see, were burning. Hagar walked slowly in the sand, alone.

9

Saturday.

The sun blazed over the sea and the beach. They came home at noon, their burning skin salty.

They showered, ate bread and butter, drank a glass of milk. They stood next to the table and Tuvia asked: "Have you written home and asked them to send you your books? If you've made up your mind, you should do something."

He was standing between the table and the wall, wearing short khaki pants and a white T-shirt, his hair wet and smooth, combed back.

"I've made up my mind," she said. And then, feeling that a few more words were necessary, she added: "But I won't write to them. I'll go down there one day and get them myself."

"Why don't you do it tomorrow?"

"Maybe I will," she said.

She put the dishes in the sink, and without washing them went to lie down. It was two o'clock.

"We'd better set the alarm," he said.

"Why?"

"We're going to the theater tonight with Yoel and his wife, have you forgotten? The play starts at nine, but I have to buy tickets."

"What time should I set it for?" She picked up the alarm clock, which was standing on the little bedside table.

"Quarter to five," he said.

She set the alarm, and he covered his body with a sheet, lay on his back, and closed his eyes.

Her head was buried in the pillow. Tuvia's hand reached for her under the sheet. She put her small hand into his hard, sinewy one, and thus they remained. Gradually Tuvia's hand relaxed. The fingers enclosing her hand slipped back. It was cool in the room. The shutters and the windows were closed. Outside a breeze blew with a soft, piercing whistle.

Tuvia was already asleep. He turned over, pulling the sheet with him. The sheet now covered only half her body, and she tugged gently at it to cover her leg, suddenly exposed to the chill of the dark room. She couldn't fall asleep. Her head buried in the pillow was wide awake. She looked at the clock but she could barely make out the figures and the hands. She switched on the little reading light. It was ten past two. She switched off the light.

In a last attempt to fall asleep, she closed her eyes and lay without moving. Her skin was sunburned and the contact with the mattress and sheets hurt her. Again she switched on the lamp, and in the dim light bathing the room she turned her head to look at her husband. The light did not disturb his sleep, and she let her bare feet down to the cold floor. Then she stood up, undid the buttons of her nightgown, and threw it onto the bed. She opened the wardrobe. The door creaked slightly, and she turned her head to the bed again. She took out a short summer dress, a scarf, and a long, narrow, brown leather bag. Then she switched off the lamp and padded bare-foot to the bathroom.

She got dressed quickly, combed her hair which was still damp from the shower, brushed her teeth, and drew a narrow black line around her eyes. At the last moment she took off the high-heeled shoes she had chosen and changed them for flat ones. She sat on the folding chair in the bathroom, and as she pushed her foot into the narrow black shoe she saw, lying in the corner, the canteen and the yellow dishcloth which she had promised Yiftach to make into a cover.

After glancing at the mirror again she returned to the bedroom. The flat felt shoes made no noise. She stood next to the bed and hesitated. Tuvia was asleep.

Without switching on the light she woke him up.

"What's up?" he asked.

"I've decided to go now," she said quickly.

"Where to?"

"To fetch the books."

"Why on earth now? You can go tomorrow. We're going out this evening. You won't be back on time. It's happened before. Your parents will want to talk to you. Anyway, there aren't any buses to Netanya yet."

"I'll be back in time. It's only quarter to three. I won't stay long. I'll take a taxi."

"Why didn't you tell me in the morning? We could have driven down together. And anyway, why do you have to go now? All of a sudden, without making any plans. What's gotten into you? Go tomorrow."

By now Tuvia was wide awake. He threw off the sheet and sat on the edge of the bed with his feet on the floor. "Why don't you switch on the light?" he asked.

"I'm going," she said. "Good-bye. Don't worry, I won't be late. Buy me a ticket." She kissed him, said, "Go back to sleep," and walked out of the room.

He lay down and wrapped the sheet tightly around him, as if he felt cold. His open eyes stared at the wall. In the dim light of the room it was hard to see himself and Hagar in the photograph hanging on the wall. But even in the dark he could see the black frame standing out against the white background.

He was tired, but he couldn't fall asleep again. He curled up in the sheet and listened to Hagar's footsteps on the paved path. He could hardly hear her, only the rustling of the rosebush which had grown onto the path told him that she had brushed against it as she passed. He heard the creaking of the gate opening and closing. Silence descended on the room again, and he snuggled deep down into the sheet.

After a while he crawled over the big double bed and lit the little reading lamp. On the bottom shelf of the bedside table he found some old magazines and an open book. Bending over, his head almost touching the floor, he turned the pages, and finally he put out the light, rolled over, and closed his eyes.

Tuvia Erlich was Yehiel Erlich's oldest son. Yehiel owned the soda factory which stood not far from the main road, surrounded by tall eucalyptus and cypress trees. Despite the lack of sunlight, lemon trees grew in the yard, and ferns climbed onto the veranda of the house which he had built at a short distance from the factory, in the same yard. The many trees cast a perpetual shade over the yard, and this, together with the black soot covering the unpainted factory walls, made it always seem dark there.

Yehiel Erlich was a heavyset man of medium height, and his eyes, hidden under black, beetle brows, seemed to look at the world sideways. He wasn't walleyed, but his irises were always in the corners of his eyes, from which he looked out obliquely at the people he was talking to, and at the crates of soda that he sold in the market. His face was lined, and there was a deep cleft in his chin. A broad mustache dipped to the corners of his mouth, and his long hair was slightly curly and usually combed back. The strange look in his eyes, the mustache that was never shaven, the flat cap which shaded his eyes and left two unruly curls above his ears, gave his face a look at once frightening and frightened.

When he was a young man, soon after he came to the village with his wife, people said his mustache was a sign of good nature. But after he bought the two horses and the cart from Stavsky, the orange grove owner for whom he worked digging basins, the attitude toward him changed. In the cafe he spoke dirty Yiddish, and to the young people born in the village he spoke the pure, fluent Hebrew he had learned in the *cheder*. In the beginning of his career as a cart-driver he worked in the surrounding Arab villages. At the same time he also learned Arabic. There was always someone sitting next to him when he drove the cart. Usually they were Arabs, getting a ride to or from work. It was Tabak who said to Kasos: "The Arab tells him the words and the sentences, and Erlich writes them down in Yiddish in his notebook. He writes Arabic in Yiddish." After that Kasos couldn't take his eyes off the fat cardboard notebook which Erlich kept in the pocket of his khaki shirt, next to his heart, and in which he wrote everything down. His work schedule, the money he owed, and the money owed to him. Later he wrote down the soda pop orders, the balance of debts, and the customers' addresses. The notebook must have been changed a number of times but it always looked like the same notebook: a brown cardboard cover, ragged at the corners, with a yellow pencil sticking out of the pages.

Not far from the village the British built an army camp. The sides of Erlich's cart rose higher, and he began transporting sacks of cement and gravel from the nearby quarries to the camp. The English paid by the load. Erlich's cart went back and forth, his horses were always sweating, and pale stripes appeared on their flanks from the lashes of his whip. He made many trips a day, but the foreman always gave him credit for five more. Nobody knew if Erlich paid him for this arrangement, or if it was simply a gesture of friendship on the part of the Englishman, who had dinner at Erlich's house every Friday night. The camp took two years to build, and when it was finished Erlich sold his horses and bought the neglected plot, whose owners had moved to Jaffa on their way to Berlin, immediately after planting the trees on it. Where he had learned the secret of making soda nobody knew. From the blocks which he transported to his yard from the army camp he built a small factory, equipped it with the necessary machines and raw materials, planted ferns under the windows, on the veranda balustrade, and began to sell. Once in a while he would go to the cafe to play dominoes. In spite of the lines etched deeply in his face, and the sprinkling of gray which had begun to invade his hair, his opponents watched him like hawks, as if he were a crook out to cheat them. And indeed, he almost always won, even though he put the dominoes on the table with frank, open movements, after prolonged deliberation and lengthy sidelong looks. His wife, Rivka, was hardly ever seen. She went to buy groceries at Tabak's once a day, and the rest of the time she stayed at home. Tuvia was their first son, but their third child. Before giving birth to him, Rivka had had two daughters, one after the other.

The first daughter got married as soon as she graduated from high school and went to live with her husband in Jerusalem. The second daughter began giving them trouble when she was still in high school, which she left after only two years. She went to work as a clerk in Tel Aviv, which was not at all to Yehiel Erlich's liking, and once he even bawled her out about it. She was still behaving in the same way when she was twenty-two years old, and from the letters he received in London from his parents, Tuvia understood that something was wrong with their relationship with the only daughter still under their care. After he had graduated from technical college, his father sent him to London to study economics and "broaden his horizons," as he called it. "You're not going to be some miserable mechanic," he said to his son when he discovered that his favorite pastime was fiddling with the machines in the factory, and fixing them when necessary. He didn't profit by it, but everyone said that he exploited even his son. Because whenever the old Morris broke down, instead of putting it in the garage, Yehiel would entrust it to the reliable hands of his son. "Saving money, eh?" Tabak would say to him, on the rare occasions when he visited the cafe, and sat squinting at the dominoes and tugging at the lock of gray hair poking out of the flat cap which he never removed from his head.

The only subject Tuvia could speak about to his father was business. But to his mother he hardly spoke at all. He liked seeing her in her clean white apron on Friday nights, in her white lace dress, lighting the candles, with an old scarf around her head. It seemed to him that only in the letters which reached him in London, was he becoming acquainted with another side of his father, an unfamiliar, rather sensitive side. "What can I say and what can I tell you," he wrote in one letter, "the house, the yard with all its trees, are empty without you." And when he met an Israeli girl called Rochelle in London and thought of marrying her, and wrote home: "What would you do if I got married one day?" Yehiel Erlich replied: "Regarding what you wrote to us, you should know that all parents want to see their children married, and to have joy of them. If you have made up your mind, please give us more details about Rochelle. What does she do? What do her parents do? If you have decided to get married, we are very happy. About details such as an apartment, etc., we can speak later. Get married, the main thing is that it shouldn't disturb your studies, and therefore I intend sending you, this coming week, a new pair of shoes."

After spending two years in London, Tuvia returned when the war broke out. He was mobilized as soon as he arrived, and the personnel classification officer, with some sixth sense, posted him to the light maintenance company permanently attached to the Givati Brigade. He would see the wounded, sweating soldiers coming back from the front while he lay underneath the battered command cars, trying to keep their engines alive with his hands for one more week, and sometimes even for one more night. Only once, at the end of the war, did he find himself under fire. With another mechanic he was attached to an assault force mounted on jeeps. They rode in the last jeep, and although they heard the men firing and shells exploding around them, they drove slowly in the relative quiet of the rear, until suddenly they received a radio communication ordering them to advance to the center of the hill. The command jeep had stalled and had been left behind by the rest of the company. Standing still, it provided an easy target for the enemy, who had not yet abandoned their dugouts on the hill. "Let's see who they hit first," Tuvia's companion laughed. But the bullets didn't even hit their wheels, and Tuvia quickly located the source of the trouble in the engine. In the repaired jeep they pursued the CO, who had changed jeeps in the course of the battle. "You got here in the nick of time," the CO roared at them, jumping into the command jeep with his team. When they were still quite close to the jeep a shell fell directly on it, killing the entire command team on the spot. Tuvia and his friend immediately dropped to the ground. But the friend was already fatally wounded. Only his head was unhurt, and his face was smooth and pure. Tuvia went up to him, and he said: "You were always lucky, you lucky bugger."

Although the war had already been over for a year when he met Hagar, she was always cross-examining him about what he had done in it, and sometimes he was glad, in the depths of his heart, that he had at least one interesting story to tell. At the same time, there was no doubt that she enjoyed the attention he paid her. The flowers, the records, the key-rings – courting manners which he could only have acquired in England. She remembered one Saturday afternoon, when she stood behind the curtain and watched what was happening in the street. The night before they had quarreled at a party given by friends, because she had danced too much, in his opinion, and he had argued too loudly, in hers. Now she saw him walking down the street with a bunch of flowers in his hands, accosting some little boys playing there. He spoke to them, but they took no notice of him. Only one boy stopped next to him, and she saw him dropping a few coins into his little hand. The boy shook his head, and Tuvia added a few more coins, and when the child was still not satisfied, he took back all the coins and replaced them with a bill. He himself turned around and took up his position behind a ficus tree, which cast its shade over a dilapidated public bench. The little boy, who was wearing a clean white shirt and short khaki pants, entered the building. Hagar abandoned her post behind the curtain and went over to the door. She heard his sandals clattering on the stairs, and then she heard the bell ring. She opened the door and the boy gave her the flowers. She wanted to give him something, but he ran away. With the bunch of flowers in her hands, she resumed her post behind the curtain. Tuvia was still standing behind the ficus tree, his hands resting on the back of the bench. He was wearing a suit and a tie. The little boy walked past him, and when Tuvia followed him he began to run. Tuvia sat down on the bench, and she took the flowers into the kitchen, where she threw the wrapping paper into the bin and looked for a note. But there was no note.

Yehiel Erlich did not live to see the marriage of his only son. In spite of his second daughter, Edna's, many suitors, it was Yehiel who found her a husband. He invited the family of an old countryman of his from Vilna, now living in Hadera, to dine with himself, his wife, Tuvia and Edna. The elderly couple came that same Friday night, but their son, who was about to complete his legal studies in Jerusalem, stayed over to spend the Sabbath with the Erlich family. The next day the young man took Edna to the movies, and amazingly enough, no cars hooted outside their house, and no stranger from Tel Aviv knocked at the door and asked: "Is Edna at home?" Two months later they were married and went to live in

Jerusalem, in a house purchased for them by their families. "My family's moving to Jerusalem," said Yehiel Erlich, and he would sometimes ask Tuvia, half humorously, half seriously: "When are you moving too?"

After seeing both his daughters settled, he bought an empty lot and began building a house for his son. In the cafe Kasos would say to him: "I hear your children are giving you joy."

"Yes, they're giving me joy," Yehiel Erlich would reply, "now we only have to wait for the lad." But at the same time, he began to get bored. He began paying frequent visits to the cafe, and although all his hair was now white, his mind was not on the game. Or in the words of Tabak: "Erlich, you're not an interesting partner any more."

One day he invited a lawyer to his house and made his will, "so there won't be any problems with the inheritance." When the document had been drawn up, which did not take long, the lawyer asked: "And what about the factory and the plot?" Erlich gave him a look which brought the black back to his hair, as in the days when he had driven his cart back and forth from the quarry to the British army camp. "The soda factory, the plot, the house, I'm selling the lot. You have to be close to your family to get some joy out of life. We're moving to Jerusalem." Like the lawyer, this was the first his wife had heard of his decision too. And when she dared to open her mouth and ask: "What's all this about?" he said again: " We're getting old, Rivka, and the place to be old is with our children, in Jerusalem." The lawyer lit a cigarette, and put it out again immediately when Erlich gave him his squinting look, accompanied by a grunt of rebuke.

"What's all this about Jerusalem?" Rivka asked again; but nobody heard her.

"We're moving to Jerusalem, and we're leaving Tuvia here. Soon the house will be built, he'll be settled too."

"Why should we leave Tuvia here? Why can't we take him with us?" asked Rivka.

"Why?" Erlich asked rhetorically, in a judicious, all-knowing tone. "Because it's not good for them to be all together. The girls will quarrel, as usual, and then it will be good to know that we've got one son here, who can come from a distance and be wise and make the peace between them. Now do you understand why?"

The lawyer didn't know what to do with his hands upon hearing this outlandish pronouncement, and he buried his eyes in the carpet.

"You can't leave Tuvia here alone, without a home, without asking him. He's our son too. Why shouldn't he be next to us too?"

"And what do you think the house I'm building him now is for?"

"But it's not finished."

"It will be finished soon. And in the meantime Tuvia can find somewhere to stay here. Even a hotel, why not? He's not a child."

"You're always forcing people," said Rivka with un-characteristic aggression, and rose to her feet.

"What are you getting up for?" said Erlich. "I've

decided. I'm not going to help him with the house any more. It's his house, let him finish it himself. And that's why he's staying here."

"Did you ask him? Why are you always jumping into things? Maybe he doesn't want the house, maybe he doesn't want to stay here at all. Have you asked him? All you do is force people, even your own son. And anyway, I can't see what's wrong with him coming with us to Jerusalem. How do you think we'll be able to live in a strange place on our own?"

Erlich waited for his wife to sit down at the table again. He didn't even see the lawyer, who had risen from his place in the meantime, and gone over to stand by the open window. "In the first place, forcing. I'm not forcing anyone. Tuvia himself would never agree to come with us. He'll want to stay here. I'm not forcing anyone. You'll see. He'll want to stay here."

"You'll persuade him," Rivka interrupted.

"Let me finish," he continued. "I won't say a word. He'll do what he wants. That's as far as forcing is concerned. And now Jerusalem. That's to say, in the second place, Jerusalem. First, Jerusalem isn't a strange place. Apart from which, we have two daughters there, and soon maybe we'll have something else too. So, firstly, I'm not forcing anyone. With me everybody does just what he pleases. On condition that it's logical, of course. And secondly, Jerusalem. . . ." He left the sentence unfinished, and as if after some strenuous effort, he leaned on the back of his chair, sighed, glanced at the lawyer standing at the window, and said to his wife: "We have a guest, why don't you bring him a cup of tea?"

At the time of this discussion, Tuvia was working in a garage in one of the nearby settlements, and when he came home that day from work, tired and unshaven, even before he had taken a shower, his mother said, "We have something to tell you." But Erlich cut in: "Let him wash up first." And after Tuvia had gone into the bathroom, he continued: "First we have to sell the house and the plot, and then we can tell him. And I haven't even found a buyer yet, so what's the point of talking. When there's nothing definite."

"You don't want to prepare him," said Rivka. "You don't want him to have time to think, to decide for himself. Because I'm positive that he'll want to leave here too, and come with us."

Erlich paced to and fro next to the frying pan and snatched a little chopped meat from the oil and onions in which it was frying. "There's nothing to tell him. He already knows whatever there is to know. He even knows that we're going to move."

"How can you be so sure?"

"There are things a person senses, and there's no need to talk about them."

"You want to surprise him, I know you."

"When I've sold everything. I'll tell him. I won't tell him what to do. He won't be surprised. There are things a person senses, and there's no need to talk about them."

When they sat down to eat she was silent, and the next

morning Erlich went off to Hadera and Tel Aviv. He was away from home for two days, and when he returned on Thursday morning, he said to Rivka: "That's that." An hour later two middle-aged men wearing suits and hats knocked at the door. Rivka showed them the house, and Erlich showed them the factory and the yard. He paced and counted aloud, measuring off the area of the plot. They said they needed time to think, but Erlich realized immediately that this was a trick, and said: "We'll be here until tomorrow morning, and after that we're leaving." At eight o'clock on Friday morning they knocked on the door again, and at Erlich's request they paid all the thousands in cash.

As soon as they had left, two moving men arrived in the yard with a truck.

"What are they doing here?" asked Rivka.

"I told you we were leaving today."

Rivka was silent, and after a few minutes she said: "I thought you were only saying that because of the buyers."

He looked at her, as if to say: "You know I never say anything I don't mean."

The movers began packing up their belongings in the big wooden crates they had brought in the truck, and when Rivka wanted to advise them, he said: "Let them be, it's their profession."

Erlich went into the factory, took out two crates of soda and left them by the gate. "We might as well take these with us," he said.

When all the cupboards were packed, and the open

shutters revealed empty walls, Tuvia was standing at the gate in his blue overalls, his lunch bag in his hand.

Erlich went up to him. "Hurry up and wash," he said, "we're moving to Jerusalem."

"What?"

"Can't you see that we're almost finished packing? Don't waste time. The more time you waste the more I'll have to pay the movers, and there's our health to consider too, the sleep we'll lose tonight."

Rivka ran up to him, embraced him, and said: "Don't ask questions, Tuvia. We're moving. Come on."

Tuvia was still confused. He advanced to the threshold of the house, and put his lunch bag down on the doorstep.

"Who says I want to move?" he said suddenly.

"We've sold the house," said Rivka.

"But I want to stay here."

"Look," said Erlich, "we're not forcing you. Just offering to take you with us."

Tuvia sat down on the step. He watched the movers arranging the crates on the back of the truck. One of the men took off his shirt and hung it on the frame. His broad shoulders, bulging out of his undershirt, glistened with sweat.

Erlich's Morris was standing outside the yard, and Tuvia heard the engine running. Then he saw his father coming into the yard and walking toward him. Tuvia stood up, wiped the beads of sweat off his forehead with his hand, and said: "Don't be angry, but I'm staying here. I've got a job, and I've got plans. I can't come with you."

His mother, who overheard him from the empty kitchen, stuck her head out of the window and said: "Tuvia," and after a short pause, "that's just what he wants. . . ."

But Tuvia didn't hear the end of the sentence, because his father said to him: "Come."

They walked toward the Morris, and one of the movers shouted at Erlich: "It's Friday, Erlich, and we still have another trip to make from Jerusalem."

"Don't worry," Erlich called back, "I'll be back soon, and then we'll go. If the Sabbath begins, you'll get extra pay. You needn't worry."

Tuvia and Erlich drove along the dirt road until they reached the main street. They passed the square and Kasos's cafe, on the way to the Arab village. Yehiel Erlich pointed out the cultivated fields to his son. "Once they were Shuster's, these fields," he said, "and I worked them." Then they turned off the road and drove between the Arab villages on the border, crossed fields, and Tuvia saw the quarries, the huge mechanical shovels digging into the rock, the workers bending over the stones and smashing them with heavy hammers. The road was paved with undressed stones, and the Morris bounced.

"You made the right decision, to stay here," said Yehiel.

The road became sandy and soft again, and the wheels plowed through it. They bypassed the orange groves, the new *moshav,* and drove down avenues of cypresses and eucalyptus trees to the army camp. Tuvia saw the long buildings with corrugated tin roofs, the brown huts, the rolls of barbed wire surrounding the huts. Tall eucalyptus trees with whitewashed trunks lined the main road which passed through the center of the camp. Soldiers swarmed around the tents, raking the stone-bordered plots, sweeping the black road, polishing the windows. There were yellow signs with red letters on the fences and sticking up at the sides of the paths. A cart piled high with corn passed along the fence of the camp. The driver was a young boy who sat on top of the pile and made no attempt to urge on the mule.

"My mare never went so slow. The road we've just traveled in the Morris, I used to cover with my horse and cart. The stones on the road inside the camp, the stones of the walls – it was me who brought them, a lot of them, anyway. With my mare. You did right to decide to stay."

They returned through plum orchards and banana plantations, and through the orange groves surrounding Noah Bulkin's yard. The roads were growing quiet and the highway too was emptying. In the gardens they occasionally caught sight of men watering flower beds with hoses, and children sitting with their mothers on the verandas. The Morris stopped outside the unfinished house which Erlich had begun to build for his son. "You'll finish building here yourself," he said to Tuvia. "And that Hagar you sometimes take out – if you think she's okay, in other words, a woman, you'll bring her here. And now we'll drive by the police station. There's something I want to show you there."

They drove up the main road, and the engine strained, emitting a gray cloud of smoke which left a twisted tail behind it, writhing in the wind. There was nobody in the street, except for the shopkeepers standing on the pavements, letting the corrugated iron doors down over their shop entrances and locking up their businesses. Noah Bulkin, wearing khaki and carrying a knapsack slung over his shoulder, walked down the street. During this period, although he had already begun building up a farm of his own, he was still working as a hired hand in one of the citrus groves. He walked slowly down the street, his head bared to the setting sun, like a man who knew he had no reason to hurry, that nobody was waiting for him. They passed a bare plot on which a couple of solitary rue had begun to grow, drove down a street crowded with low houses, one touching the other, and reached the police station.

In the station yard too the Sabbath eve atmosphere was already making itself felt. The earth underneath the pine trees which shaded the yard was clean and raked. Two white lines shone at the sides of the drive leading to the entrance of the building. There were a couple of bicycles leaning against the gate, and prisoners' heads peeped out of little barred windows on the ground floor. A last taxi drove down the road. A bare field with a knoll rising in its center stretched along the main road next to the police station. Erlich parked the Morris on the side of the road, opposite the knoll.

He switched off the engine and stepped outside. Tuvia got out after him and followed him up the side of the hillock. When Erlich reached the top, he took off his flat cap. Tuvia looked at his father's hair, which was white with vigorous strands woven into a kind of coarse tangle that shone with a peculiar brilliance. His father's face looked a little different now that he had taken off his cap. It was bronzed, with a broad red band on the top of his lined forehead, in the place which was always shaded by the peak of his cap. His look suddenly seemed direct, and he looked without squinting at his son climbing up toward him. The sun was about to sink. The field and the side of the knoll were already in the shade. Only on the summit a few pale sunbeams still glimmered.

A dry, uprooted thorn bush attached itself to Tuvia's pants. He stood next to his father, bent over, pulling the thorns out of his pants and listening. "Two *dunams* of this big field belong to me. From this hillock and all the way to the road. I'm leaving you this too. The papers are all in order. They're sure to build around here. But this area is right next to the road. If you want to do something, this is a good place to do it."

In the distance they could see the cypresses and the Persian lilac trees on the border of the neighboring village. Their crowns too were lit up by the sun. But now the light was slowly withdrawing, from treetop to treetop. And by the time they reached the Morris, everything was already a mass of gray shadow.

Yehiel Erlich climbed into the cab on the passenger's side. "I'm tired," he said to his son, "you drive." Tuvia started the engine, and Erlich threw his cap down on the seat. He didn't put it on again.

The movers worked quickly. They shoved the crates up against the cab of the truck, stacked them one on top of the other, and crowded them together. Then they threw ropes over the stacked crates, sliding them through the wooden slats of the frame at the sides of the truck.

"It took more than a few minutes," said one of the men who had taken off his shirt.

"Never mind, you'll have less work to do in Jerusalem," said Erlich as he got out of the Morris. "Unloading is always easier."

There was a bottle of cold water in the second man's hand. The load was already shipshape, tied down with stout ropes to the iron hooks sticking out of the sides of the truck.

Rivka, a large basket in her hand, was standing at the gate, in the broad shadow cast by the ficus tree. In her other hand she was holding her parents' family portrait in its brown carved frame, the figures with their dresses touching the ground and their long beards blurred as if with age. Behind her, next to the two crates of soda, stood Tuvia.

"The new owners are only arriving at the end of next week," said Erlich. "You can stay here until you find something."

"And where is he going to have dinner tonight?" asked Rivka.

Erlich went up to the movers sitting in the cab of the truck. He gave them a sheet of paper. "You can get going," he said. "The address is written here. We'll follow you in the Morris."

The truck moved off, and dense smoke mingled with the dust kicked up by the wheels. They could still hear the engine straining to get out of the sand onto the main road when Yehiel came up to Tuvia, shook his hand and pressed his shoulders to his chest. Rivka handed the basket and the old picture to her husband, went up to Tuvia, kissed him, and only began to cry when she was on her way to the Morris.

The two crates of soda were still standing next to the gate. Erlich loaded them quickly onto the back of the Morris, started the engine, and drove off. Rivka looked back and saw her son standing next to the fence in his stained overalls, in the shadow which covered his face.

Tuvia stood there next to the gate, gazing after the receding Morris. The tailgate was open. His father had forgotten to shut it. It flapped and banged, and when the van had disappeared from sight he went back into the yard. He picked his lunch bag up from the step, opened the door and entered the empty house. The shutters were open and cool air streamed toward him from all directions.

He lay awake, curled up under the starched sheet. The room was dark.

His back was red from the sun which had burned it that morning on the beach. The starched sheet hurt him.

The alarm clock rang. It was quarter to five. The ringing went on and on in the dark room, but he didn't jump up to stop it.

He lay under the sheet and let the ringing stop on its own.

When the alarm stopped ringing it seemed to him that

the darkness in the room was blacker. And even the ticking of the clock was stilled.

10

He went on lying in bed a few minutes longer, and then he switched on the light and went to shower and shave. It was quiet in the house, and apart from the splashing of the water in the sink and the scraping of the razor on his skin, there wasn't a sound to be heard. He got dressed, and when he went out into the street it was already twilight. There was a light on in Sarah and Simcha Strauss's house, and the streetlights cast pale patches on the sand.

There weren't many people waiting in line outside the theater, and he bought four tickets and went home. Hagar wasn't back yet. He switched on the radio, sat in the kitchen, and read the newspaper. He was hungry.

Although the light was on in the kitchen, it seemed to him that he was sitting in great darkness. He stood up, took some cold meatballs out of the refrigerator, and put the kettle on the gas. Then he put on the lights on the front veranda and in the living room. Now the whole house was lit up.

He ate the meatballs standing up at the marble counter next to the sink, and made himself a cup of coffee. Then he took a few cookies out of the cupboard, and sat down at the table again. The radio was on, but he was reading and didn't hear it.

The time was already half past seven. He reset the alarm clock and drank another cup of coffee. Hagar still wasn't back. "She left at three," he said to himself. "An hour to Netanya, and an hour back. Another hour, let's say two, at her parents'. Four hours. She should have been back by now. Even if she took the bus." When he had finished drinking his coffee he heard footsteps on the path. He went to the door, waited a moment, and opened it.

Carmela and Yoel were walking up the path toward him. He showed them into the living room, opened the sideboard, took out glasses and filled them with wine.

"Have you got the tickets?" asked Yoel.

"Yes," said Tuvia, "I only got back a few minutes ago."

"Where's Hagar?" asked Carmela.

"She should be back any minute now," said Tuvia and took a sip of wine. "She went to see her parents in Netanya."

"Is it true that she wants to teach next year?" asked Carmela.

"Yes. That's why she went. To get her books so she can prepare for the exams. She did all the courses but in the end she didn't sit for the exams. She hasn't got a certificate."

Carmela stood up. She hadn't touched her wine. She walked over to the bookcase and looked at the books.

Her hair was long and hung loose on her shoulders. She was broad, and her face was round and plump, with smooth skin and smiling eyes. She looked young, unlike Yoel, who despite his height walked and sat with a permanent stoop, whose hair was going gray at his temples, and who had a silver tooth which showed when he laughed. Above the bookcase there was a picture, a pen and ink drawing of a fisherman on the bank of a river. On the blue cloth spread over the low table stood an empty vase.

"Where did you leave the kids?" asked Tuvia.

"Yoel's mother's looking after them."

It was eight o'clock. Hagar still hadn't come home.

"I hope nothing's happened to her," said Tuvia, in an offhand tone, in order to break the silence which had fallen on the room.

"Don't worry, she'll come. Women are always late."

Carmela sat down next to the table. "It'll be a good thing if Hagar begins teaching. Since Esther Schmerling died our son's had a different teacher every week, it's really impossible. Well, never mind, the summer holidays are beginning."

"It'll be better for her too," said Tuvia. "It's hard on her being alone in the house all day."

"He understands," said Carmela to her husband.

Yoel was silent. He looked away, staring into the empty hall and the entrance to the bedroom, and then he said: "But you don't understand, I think."

Tuvia got up and opened the front door. He stood on the threshold. "I don't know what got into her today," he said. He shut the door slowly, as if he didn't want them to hear it closing, and returned to the table.

"You can go ahead, if you like," said Tuvia. "You don't have to stay on my account. I'll wait for her. We'll come later."

"We'll wait with you," said Carmela. "There's no hurry, we've still got time."

"You'd better go," said Tuvia. "I don't want you to be late because of me. I'll wait. If worse comes to worst we'll take the jeep."

"Take the jeep? On Saturday night? When you can walk down the street with her like a human being?" said Carmela.

Tuvia poured Yoel another glass of wine, but he couldn't go on sitting next to them. He went to the bathroom, combed his hair and washed his face. When he returned to the living room he looked at his watch. It was half past eight. Hagar still wasn't back. There wasn't a footstep to be heard on the garden path.

"Go on," he said, "I'll wait."

"Come with us," said Carmela. "She probably went straight to the theater because she saw that it was getting late. There's no point in you waiting here."

Tuvia didn't reply, and when Yoel and Carmela rose to their feet, he rose too, opened the door, and followed them out. They walked along the main road, passed the deserted bus station next to the square, and continued walking down the pavement thronged with people. The shop windows were lit up, and neon lights shone above the new cafe that had opened on the corner of the street where the theater was located. Because of the electric lights flooding the street it was impossible to see any stars that might have been in the sky. And the stifling heat that suddenly descended on them made it seem as if the sky was covered with a thick layer of barren summer clouds.

When they reached the theater, after stopping to greet various people on the way, it was ten to nine. Everybody began going in while they stood to one side, under the billboard advertising the movies that were showing that week.

"Go in," said Tuvia.

"There's still time," said Yoel. "You'll see, she'll come."

"Maybe her parents delayed her," said Tuvia. "It's happened before."

They heard the first bell. Tuvia took the tickets out of his wallet and handed two of them to Yoel. They went on waiting next to him until the third bell rang. "Go on, go in," he said to them. "Never mind, we'll wait a little longer," said Carmela. But a moment or two later she added, "Don't worry," and they went in.

There was nobody left outside the theater, apart from a few latecomers hurrying up to hand their tickets to the usher, who was leaning against the side of the door. Tuvia remained alone under the billboard, with the naked neon light and the silent fleet of cars parked in the street. The usher left the doorway and joined Tuvia on the pavement. "Waiting for the wife, eh?" he said. Tuvia smiled at him, and when the usher returned to his post, he stepped off the neon-lit pavement and began walking down the road toward the bus stop. Suddenly the street seemed deserted, and apart from a group of children running up and down and an elderly couple walking their dog, all he could see were the tree trunks lining the road. He walked along between them, and then he turned back.

He looked at his watch. It was only quarter past nine. He saw that it was already dark in the hall. The usher closed the door and went to sit on a bench next to the wall. Tuvia went on pacing up and down the brightly lit pavement, until in the end he stepped off the curb, took a few steps down the street, and stopped in the shadow of the hedge surrounding the facade of the building. It was quiet in the street, and it was hot. He was thirsty.

The Morris arrived at the new apartment in Jerusalem half an hour before the truck. They opened up the apartment, and since there wasn't even a chair to sit on, they returned to the Morris and waited for the truck. When it arrived the movers quickly unloaded the crates, carried them into the apartment, took out the furniture, received their pay and their bonus for working on the Sabbath, and left. Erlich and his wife went to spend the night with their eldest daughter. That same evening they paid a visit to Edna, who was living in Rehavia, too, and the next day, with the help of both their daughters and their husbands, they fixed up their new apartment, which was situated on the border of Romema, not far from the Mahane Yahuda marketplace.

Erlich no longer worked, nor did he make much use of the Morris, which stood on the street corner, abandoned, until people thought that it didn't belong to anyone. They lived on the monthly interest they received from the bank, and spent their time walking around the Jerusalem streets. Rivka liked climbing Mount Zion, passing the old Yemin Moshe quarter and going down to the ruins of Abu Tur, which reminded her of the ruined Arab village to the east of their old home. Erlich haunted the marketplace. He persuaded Rivka to do her shopping there, and he spent hours roaming around the alleys alone, late at night and in the morning too. They would wake up early in the morning and set out. Erlich liked wandering about among the crates of onions and vegetables, the heavy meathooks, and the paper bags scattered over the narrow streets. The torn bags mingled with the dry husks of the corn and rotting fruit which had fallen from the crates.

"There's money to be made here," said Erlich one day, putting on his old khaki trousers and pulling the flat cap down on his head again. He checked the engine of the Morris, started it, and drove to the market. When he returned at the end of the day, he said that he had hired the van out to a hauling company. "A person has to do something," he said. The truth was that he didn't have to do anything, but nevertheless, he got up every night and drove with the driver from the hauling company to one of the surrounding villages, helped him to load the vegetable crates, or the chicken cages, onto the van, and returned with him before dawn to the market, to unload the crates and distribute them among the stall owners.

Once again he began coming home late and demanding food. When he suffered an attack of high blood pressure while unloading the van he took no notice, and after the second attack they brought him home in an ambulance, and he was forced to stay in bed.

His blood pressure did not go down, and everyone knew that it could happen at any minute. His daughters came to see him every day. Tuvia came every Saturday morning. One Saturday he came with Hagar. His sisters looked at her coldly, and she put the bar of chocolate she had brought on the table without saying anything. Erlich hardly spoke, and although his eyes burned he seemed to exist in a twilight zone between life and death. The uncertain situation, the blood pressure which shot over the highest measure on the doctor's instrument, started getting on their nerves. His daughters began to react with impatience to his few requests and to resent it when Rivka pressed them to visit as often as they could. He hung on like this for nearly six months. And then, one Sunday evening, when the representative of the hauling company came to give Rivka the monthly check, without any of his children at his side, he died.

After his parents left for Jerusalem, Tuvia stayed in the only hotel in the town. There were no more than eight rooms in the hotel, only four of which were regularly occupied, and in order to add to his income the proprietor had opened a dress shop on the ground floor, next to the narrow reception hall. In addition to Tuvia there were two Arabs who worked for a local farmer staying in the hotel, and a middle-aged engineer employed by the government, who had come to supervise the construction of a new network of roads. Tuvia came there only to sleep. He worked overtime at the garage where he was employed and invested the money in the building of his house. For lunch he would buy two sandwiches and a cup of coffee at the stand next to the garage, and every evening, after taking a shower at the hotel, he would have dinner at Kasos's cafe together with Noah Bulkin.

Around this time Communist Party posters began to appear every morning on the electricity poles, and at Leibowitz's barbershop suspicion fell on Noah Bulkin. "I saw you with my own eyes, you and your bicycle," Leibowitz said to him once, while spraying his face with his favorite rose-scented aftershave lotion. "You and your crooked eyeglasses," retorted Bulkin. But Leibowitz stood his ground. He sprayed another jet right into Bulkin's eyes, and then he said with a sneer: "A private plot of your own. And a whole henhouse full of chickens. And that's all you've got to do in the mornings? Stick posters on electric poles? Oh, you capitalist communist!" But Bulkin only sniffed, and breathed in the scent of the roses.

Nevertheless, Tuvia became friendly with Bulkin during this period. When they were tired of sitting in the cafe and watching the old men playing dominoes, or listening to Kasos's gramophone playing the same old squeaking violin tunes which lingered on as a memento of Alexander, they would go to the cinema together. Once a week he would go to Tel Aviv to see Hagar, and from time to time he would go to Jerusalem to visit his parents and his sisters. In the meantime Hagar's parents had moved to Netanya, taking their diamond-polishing plant with them. Tuvia helped them fix up their apartment, hammering nails into the walls and putting up new blinds. This endeared him to her parents, but Hagar suddenly said: "It's not your job. You shouldn't have done it." However, when they decided to get married, her father gave Tuvia a big loan, and the building of the house was completed ahead of schedule.

His sisters' telegram did not arrive until Monday morning. It said: "Father passed away. Come immediately." But Tuvia had already gone out, and he only received the telegram in the evening, when he came home from work. The hotel owner said to him in a subdued voice, as if he were trying to hide something, "A telegram came for you." The telegram was open, and Tuvia asked him, standing in the dress shop which was still open, "Why didn't you call me at work?" The hotel owner was silent, and his wife said: "We didn't want to alarm you." After that she accompanied him to his room and told him that there was hot water in the shower. Tuvia threw his overalls onto a chair and went straight to the bathroom. He took a shower, but he didn't shave. He packed his toilet articles in a small bag, and was about to set out, when there was a knock at the door. There were three people standing in the corridor. Tabak, Noah Bulkin, and the hotel owner's wife.

They were dressed in their best, and Tabak grasped Tuvia by the shoulders and drew him toward him. He wanted to say something, but his voice was choked and unintelligible. Noah Bulkin said straight out: "Tuvia, we're coming with you to the funeral tomorrow. Kasos may come too." Tuvia, unshaven and heavy-eyed, was embarrassed, and he smiled lopsidedly. He held Tabak and tried to embrace him, and then he held out his hand to Noah Bulkin. The hotel owner's wife stood behind them, looking impatient. When they turned away, she said: "Another telegram came for you." She held out the folded blue slip of paper to him, and then she took two steps backward, leaned against the wall, and waited to hear what it said. Tuvia opened the telegram with trembling fingers. "According to will, funeral to take place in the village. Arriving immediately. Wait for us." He was silent for a moment, and then he said: "I'm going anyway." But Tabak was more logical: "They may be on their way here already. Wait." They sat in his room and from time to time the hotel owner's wife brought them tea. Nobody spoke. When supper time approached, Tabak and Noah Bulkin left him. Tabak went home. Bulkin went to Kasos's cafe. After a while Bulkin returned with two covered cooking pots. "From Kasos," he said. There were baked potatoes and meat in the pots and hot coffee in the thermos. "I'm not hungry," said Tuvia. "You have to be strong now," said Bulkin, but by the time Tuvia tasted the potatoes they were already cold. At midnight Kasos and his wife came too, and only after they had gone did he get to bed. When he was left alone he couldn't fall asleep, and he said to himself: "I should have gone to Jerusalem." And in fact, the family did not arrive until the next morning.

The sun was in their eyes, and Friedman the grave digger's mare was nervous. She blinked her runny eyes, jerked her head up and down, and stamped on the road with her rusty horseshoes.

The sisters supported their mother, who was dressed in black, her face crumpled and her eyes weeping. Tabak and Kasos stood by Tuvia, who was wearing a white hat with a black band on his bowed head. He refused to allow anyone else to fill the grave, and shoveled the red earth in all by himself. After that the cantor sang again, and Tuvia began to cry. Quietly, soundlessly, the tears flowed from his eyes. His mother freed herself from her daughters' arms, went up to him, and embraced him. Hagar walked in the procession at their sides, but when they reached the grave, she went and stood next to Noah Bulkin. "I don't like funerals," she said to him. Bulkin took off his cap and said: "Nobody likes it. But it has to be done." A low mound of earth rose on the grave, and one of the gravediggers stuck a white wooden sign with black letters on it into the mound. Hagar went up to Tuvia and his mother and took their hands in hers.

They sat shivah in Jerusalem, in their mother's apartment. There were no new friends and neighbors to pay them condolence calls, but a few delegates came from the village, and Hagar came every day with her parents.

They got married two months later, in Netanya, and went to live in the hotel. A few weeks after that they moved into their new house, although the walls were not yet painted and the doors of the built-in cupboards had not yet been fitted. There were shutters on the windows but no window frames or windowpanes. All these jobs were completed when they were already living in the house. "Aren't you cold?" the workers asked them. But it was summer, and the breeze which came in through the slats of the shutters at night caressed their skin and their souls.

"Mother's miserable all alone in that big apartment," Tuvia's sister wrote to him. "Sometimes she babysits for Chaya's little girl, and sometimes she comes to me and makes Friday night dinner for us. But the apartment's too big for her and she's lonely. I think we should do something." Tuvia and Hagar understood that his sisters were hinting that they should invite their mother to come and stay with them. And Hagar wrote: "We would be very happy to have her with us for a while. Soon the workers will finish fitting all the doors and windows. And then they'll have to tile the walls in the kitchen and the bathroom. The garden's already looking lovely, Tuvia works in it every Saturday. We've planted fruit trees, and flowers next to the veranda. As soon as the house is ready we'll invite Mother to come to us for a long stay. It's summer now, and the weather here is very pleasant. I think she'll be glad to come."

The reply to this letter came after the shutters and window frames in their house had already been painted pale green, and the workers were coming every morning to lay the white tiles in the bathroom. "Mother's feeling better now," wrote Edna. "She's met a distant relative of Chaya's husband, a childless widower, and they go out together. They go to listen to lectures and to see plays in Yiddish, when there are any. Whenever Chaya asks her to come and babysit she comes. But she has to be asked. Maybe we'll all come and visit you over Rosh Hashana. And Mother may stay on for the whole of the holiday season."

Two weeks after a Sabbath visit Tuvia and Hagar paid the family in Jerusalem, during which they had also met the childless widower, a tall, thin, shriveled man who worked as a clerk in the municipality, they received another letter: "Mother's getting married. Both of us think it will be good for her. It's hard for a woman of her age to be alone, especially in a big, empty apartment. Now she'll have someone to look after, and she'll feel better." Rivka and her new husband spent the holiday season with Tuvia and Hagar in their new house. Rivka's new husband proved to be an interesting man to talk to. His voice trembled slightly, but he had an opinion about everything under the sun, and when they went for a walk together in the surrounding countryside it turned out that he had once spent the winter in a neighboring village, working as a carpenter in the citrus-packing plant. On the wall over the kitchen cupboard hung a picture of Tuvia's parents. Rivka and Yehiel Erlich. One evening his mother's new husband looked at the picture, and said: "I think I saw him once. He was a cart-driver, right?"

"Hasn't she come yet?"

Yoel came out of the hall, crossed the lighted pavement, and stopped next to the row of cars parked in the street. He saw Tuvia standing in the shadow of the tall bushes planted round the theater.

Tuvia turned round and saw Yoel's silhouette. "Hasn't she come yet?" Yoel asked again.

"You shouldn't have come out," said Tuvia.

"Come on in. We can leave a ticket with the usher for Hagar when she arrives. Why should you miss the play? Anyway you're not accomplishing anything by standing here alone in the dark."

A taxi drove past them and stopped outside the theater. Three people got out of it, a couple and a single man. They made haste to pay the driver and handed their tickets to the usher.

The taxi disappeared, leaving the street deserted between its silent guard of parked cars. "Okay, let's go in," said Tuvia.

"So she didn't come?" asked the usher.

"She'll be late," said Tuvia, giving him Hagar's ticket. "Keep it, and let her in when she arrives."

"I don't need the ticket," said the usher, handing it back to Tuvia without tearing off the stub. "I know her."

As they passed between the rows of people they heard the voices of the actors, dressed up as wretched down-and-outs, moving around the stage.

"She's always doing this," Tuvia blurted out as they sat down next to Carmela.

"Never mind," whispered Yoel, "these things happen."

They sat in silence and watched the play.

From time to time Tuvia turned his head back and

shifted in his seat. He was tired and he couldn't concentrate on what the actors were saying. The sets were drab too, and did not catch his attention. He didn't understand the clamorous applause which broke out at the end of the first act, when the curtains slowly closed and met in the middle of the stage. "She won't come now," he whispered quickly to Yoel sitting next to him, looking at the empty stage and clapping his hands.

Together with the rest of the audience they went outside for the intermission. As they passed the usher, Tuvia said to him: "I don't think she'll be coming." But nevertheless, the three of them left the theater and walked down the street as far as the billboard on the corner. A young motorcyclist drove past them, but the street was deserted.

They were late for the second act too, but suddenly Tuvia began to concentrate on what was happening on the stage. A father was visiting his son in a jailyard. Afterward, Tuvia remembered one sentence which the father said to his son: "No one will ever give me back the peace of mind you robbed me of." The son was silent and the father leaned against the post of the wire fence.

At the end of the play he joined in the applause, but when they went out into the street he retreated into silence.

"We'll walk you home," said Carmela.

"There's no need," said Tuvia. "She probably came back late and stayed at home."

They walked among the crowds thronging the street. A few cars, their headlights on, nosed their way slowly through the people, who were pushed to the sides of the road. Next to the square, between the taxi stand and Kasos's well-lit cafe, they stopped.

"Good night," said Carmela.

"That's it. So tomorrow morning it's back to work again. We have to finish with those *Tnuva* vans," said Yoel. He shook Tuvia's hand and then put his arm around Carmela's shoulder. They walked away.

Alone Tuvia entered the street. There was no one else in it. Sarah and Simcha Strauss's house was dark. So was his.

He entered the yard through the big gate. Dewdrops glittered on the windows of the jeep. Hagar wasn't back yet. He took the key from the windowsill and went inside. On the table in the living room stood the wineglasses. Two empty glasses and one half full – Carmela's. He drank a glass of cold water in the kitchen, and then he went into the bedroom and took the cover off the bed. Before he lay down to sleep, he took the theater ticket with the stub, Hagar's ticket, out of his pocket and put it on the table.

I I

The sun blazed. There was nobody in the square. Only the tall concrete column rose forlornly in its center. The door of Kasos's cafe too was shut. In the distance, at the end of the street, next to the broad avenue of cypresses, she saw two children in white shirts. They were walking on the pavement in the direction of the soccer field.

She walked slowly, but sweat was beginning to collect in her armpits. Next to the police station, at the bend in the road, she went to stand in the shade of a eucalyptus tree. There were two soldiers and an elderly couple standing next to the tree. The soldiers took turns leaning against the tree trunk. Occasionally one of them went to stand in the road to try to hitch a ride.

A cab stopped.

"Haifa," called the cabdriver. The old couple got in immediately, and Hagar asked: "Can you take me as far as Netanya?"

"Get in," he said.

The soldiers remained standing where they were. The driver looked at them. "There's one more place," he said, "anyone interested?" The soldiers conferred, and the cabbie began pulling away slowly. Suddenly one of them came running after the cab. The cabbie stopped and the soldier got in.

"Haifa?" he asked.

"Shut the door well," said the cabbie to the soldier, who squeezed in next to Hagar on the back seat.

The cab moved quickly, and Hagar examined the soldier sitting next to her. He took off his green beret and put it on his knees. His face was in shadow, squeezed into the corner of the cab. Hagar noticed the dried sweat on his tanned face, in contrast with his neatly pressed uniform. He closed his eyes and tried to fall asleep. She remembered the soldier she had seen next to the Arab village. His stained, patched uniform like a natural continuation of his weary face. She remembered his slightly crooked nose, his ungainly walk. It was hard for her to imagine him in other clothes. Without his equipment, without his steel helmet. He too was supposed to get leave today. He'd said so yesterday. Would he too be wearing a clean uniform now? What color was his beret? Green? Black? Red? Where would he go to spend his short leave today?

The soldier woke up and took a cigarette out of the packet in his shirt pocket. He opened the window, lit the cigarette, and blew out smoke. But the old woman said to him: "My husband's ill. Would you mind not smoking?" The soldier took a long drag, stubbed out the burning tip of the cigarette, and put it back in the pack. She couldn't remember if her soldier smoked too.

At exactly four o'clock the cab stopped in the center of Netanya, and Hagar got out and went to her parents'. The town was unfamiliar to her. She was already grownup when they moved there. She walked along the pavement parallel to the beach, and the waves glittered in her eyes. Then she turned into an avenue shaded by cypresses and pines. Something stopped her from going straight to their house. She went into a cafe and sat down at a table overlooking the street.

The waiter came up to her.

"Coffee," said Hagar.

"Iced?"

"No, plain black coffee."

She waited for the coffee to stop steaming before taking her first sip. Then she turned her eyes to the street. She drank slowly, as if she didn't want to finish the coffee and get up.

"Did you come alone?" they would ask her at home.

She would keep quiet, put her bag down on the kitchen table, and say: "Can't you see?"

"We can see," her father would say.

He would sit down at the table, put on his glasses, and read the Saturday paper. It would seem to her that the wrinkles around his eyes were deeper, and only his hair never lost its black color. He would be wearing a white shirt and shorts. The shirt collar would be open, but there would be gold cuff links on the cuffs. He wouldn't wait for a reply, and he would hide his face in the newspaper again.

"We wanted to come this morning," she would lie, "but Tuvia was busy. He had to go around to his partner's. They promised someone to have his car ready on Sunday, and they had to work on it. Afterward they did the accounts. He came home at lunchtime, worn out. And he went to sleep."

"Do you want something to drink?" her mother would ask, and she would hear the gas hissing under the kettle.

"How are you?" she would ask. But they wouldn't answer her. Her mother's hair would be done, she would have it in a black net until the evening.

"It was hot today," she would say, and immediately add: "Do you know what I came for? We've decided that I'm going to start working next year."

"Working?" her mother would say.

"At what?" her father would put in.

"I've come for my books. I'm going to take my teaching exams in the summer. And maybe next year I'll start teaching at the school. They need a teacher there, and I need something to do." She would speak quickly.

"How's Tuvia?" her father would say.

"All right."

"Actually, that's a good idea," he would add. "But you should think about a family as well. Getting married isn't enough."

The coffee would already be on the table, and next to it a tray with assorted cookies and apples. Her father would put the newspaper down and peel an apple.

"Parents always nag," her father would go on. "It's nothing to get upset about. They're never satisfied. First they want their children to be educated. Then they want them to have families. In other words, to bring children into the world. That's the way things are."

"So I've come to get my books," Hagar would repeat. She would take a bite of the apple cake, take a sip of coffee to get rid of the taste of the cake, and say: "You've worried enough. Why should you suffer because of our problems?"

"Some parents know how to keep their mouths shut. We've never been good at that."

"Leave her alone," her mother would say. "She's hardly arrived and you're getting started with her already."

Afterward they would go to look for the books and

notebooks. When she had left home she put them in the closet in her room. Where were they now? Had they moved them into the moldy storage loft over the bathroom?

A young couple came into the cafe and sat down next to Hagar. The waiter turned to them, but Hagar beckoned him with her hand. She paid the bill, picked up her bag, smoothed down her hair and left. She walked along the shady avenue, and turned left into one of the side streets. The entrance to the building was decorated with two creepers. She walked up to the second floor and knocked on the door. She knocked twice, but there was no reply. She pressed the bell. The ring echoed, penetrated into the rooms, but there was no reply. She rummaged in her bag and found the key to the apartment. She glanced around quickly, as if she felt uneasy about something, and opened the door. The shutters were closed. She tiptoed to her parents' bedroom. The door was closed. She stopped outside it and reached for the doorknob. Slowly she turned it, and opened the door. The hinges were oiled and they didn't creak.

The room was empty. The bed was made. The closet was shut. The books on the night table next to the bed were closed too. Her parents weren't at home. She felt faintly disappointed and sat down on the bed. Her legs and back ached with weariness. She lay down, and the darkness made her close her eyes. For a moment she forgot herself and fell asleep. But immediately she started up into a sitting position again. She left the bedroom and went to the kitchen. She put her bag on the table and looked into the sink. There were two cups and saucers in it. There were black coffee dregs in the cup nearest the tap. She went into the bathroom and washed her face. On the hooks behind the door she saw her parents' damp swimsuits.

Refreshed by the cold water, she went back into the kitchen. She put the kettle on to boil and in the meantime she washed the few dishes in the sink. Transparent drops of water dripped off her wet hands. She felt like having something cold to drink. She switched off the gas and went over to the refrigerator. She found some stewed plum juice and drank a few spoonfuls. Then she went to her old room. Her bed was in its old place under the window. But her wardrobe was full of bed linen, sheets and pillowcases, old blankets. The books were no longer there. Her old desk was empty too, although the blue globe standing on the corner was clean and free of dust. A white lace curtain covered the window. Next to it hung a gray photograph: she and Tuvia, next to the main road, against a background of the eucalyptus and the garage.

She remembered that there was no picture of her parents hanging on the walls of her own house. Only one of Tuvia's parents, and suddenly she felt Yehiel Erlich's eyes fixed on her with their strange, sly squint.

She returned to the bathroom and looked up at the loft. It was covered with a coarse curtain. She needed a ladder to climb up and look inside it, to find her books. But the ladder was on the balcony, and she felt faint at the thought of dragging it to the bathroom, setting it up, climbing the rungs and rummaging through the piles of junk in the close, stifling air of the loft. She returned to the kitchen, sat down at the table and went on sipping the plum juice.

She washed the glass, dried it and put it back in the cupboard. Then she opened one of the drawers in the dresser, took out paper and a pencil, and wrote a short note to her parents. It was half past five.

When she returned to the avenue she felt faint again, and she only recovered when she reached the street parallel to the beach where a refreshing breeze was blowing from the sea. The waves glittered in the sun and a muffled roar, of the waves and the crowds, rose in her ears. At the central bus station she thought she saw her parents coming out of a small cafe. She turned her face to a display window full of dresses, lingered there for a minute, and went on walking.

At the Tel Aviv bus stop she paused but she didn't buy a ticket at the booth, and after standing in line for a few minutes, she suddenly walked away. She walked along the platform, and then she went back to the booth, bought a ticket, returned to the line and took up her place at the end of it. "You were standing behind me," said a woman at the front of the line. "It doesn't matter," said Hagar, "thank you."

The road wound between the dunes beside the sea. But the buildings lining the road grew imperceptibly taller, and suddenly she was in Tel Aviv. The bus drove slowly into the maze of the central bus station. People rose from their places and pushed toward the door. Hagar remained seated. Her head was pressed against the window.

"Aren't you getting off?" asked the driver.

He looked into the mirror set above the window in front of him. He smiled. The bus was already empty. She was embarrassed. She smiled, but didn't say anything. She stood up, straightened her skirt, and stepped onto the pavement. The bus drove into the parking lot.

All of a sudden she was in the middle of a crowd. People streamed past her. They all seemed to know where they were going. She moved slowly, but the stream into which she had been cast thrust her forward. Where to, she didn't know. She stopped, stepped off the sidewalk, and stood between two cars parked at the side of the road. Then she went down an alley which led her toward the railway station. From there, by a narrow side street, she reached Allenby Street, and joined the crowds streaming toward Mograbi. People jostled her, and her feet were wet with sweat.

She wanted to rest, but the benches lining the sidewalks were full. Finally she found a bench in a boulevard crossing Allenby Street. There was a woman in a black dress and a hat decorated with flowers sitting on the edge of the bench. A gilt-topped cane was leaning against the slats of the bench, and the old woman's hand was clutching a leather leash attached to the collar of a well-groomed, curly white puppy.

On the other side of the boulevard dance music blared from a cellar. It was getting dark, and boys and girls filed into the passage at the entrance to the cellar. Two bouncers stood at the doorway taking money from the youngsters coming to dance. Hagar knew one of the tunes they were playing, and she hummed it silently to herself.

"What do you do in Tel Aviv? Hang around next to Mograbi. On the promenade."

This remark, which the soldier had made beside the stone wall after refusing to take the canteen and giving it to Yiftach, sprang up inside her.

She had lost the image of his face – she didn't know if she would recognize him if she saw him in the street.

She stood up. The old woman next to her remained seated while the little dog scurried around her feet. Again she was part of the crowd. People streamed past her in different directions, brushing against her body. She stepped into the road, and walked parallel to the sidewalk. Next to the traffic lights she saw a group of young men clustered around a stall selling drinks. Two soldiers were drinking soda. They looked at her. She didn't know them, but without her willing it, her eyes rested on them. One of them smiled at her, but the traffic lights changed and she crossed the street.

The two soldiers walked past her. At first she saw them whole, but then they were gradually swallowed up by the crowd, and only their colored berets bobbed up and down among the heads of the people, focusing her eyes on them.

"What do you do in Tel Aviv? Hang around next to Mograbi. On the promenade."

Again the words rose up inside her. She wanted to go home. She looked at her watch. It was a quarter past eight. Late. Even if she took a cab. She walked down Allenby to the sea.

The felafel, shishlik and kebab stands whetted her appetite. A smell of frying onions assailed her nostrils. Pale smoke rose from meat grilling on the charcoal fires. The sea was stormy. The sound of the waves drowned out the commotion of the street. She walked past the benches facing the sea. She saw the lights of Jaffa penetrating the waves, the lamps of a distant fishing boat. A car drove slowly along the road next to the sidewalk. When Hagar stood still for a moment, the car stopped too. There were two men sitting inside it, and one of them stared at her. He made a gesture with his hand. She did not react. The car drove on.

Between the little restaurants and stalls were the gaming alleys. Men pushed their way in, crowded round the rifles, the targets, the balls. At the entrance to one of the alleys she saw two sailors gambling with cards and dice. The cards were lying on an upended barrel. A short, skinny, unshaven man shook the dice in a round tin cup.

"Place your bets!" he shouted.

The sailors put down bills on the upturned cards, the skinny man threw the dice on the barrel. One of the sailors picked up the money. There were pictures of playing cards on the dice.

At the corner of the promenade she saw another upended barrel with cards lying faceup on its surface. She walked past it quickly, and turned up a narrow side street leading to Mograbi.

"Place your bets! One lira! Two! Five! Place your bets! Your luck's laughing today!"

Shortly afterward she heard a cry: "Police!"

She stopped and turned her head. The man standing next to the barrel had turned it quickly over. He put the dice in his pocket and divided the money among the gamblers.

Suddenly she began to run. She saw two women walking slowly in the middle of the alley. When they saw her running, they disappeared quickly into the dark stairwells of the buildings lining the alley. She looked behind her again. There was nobody behind her and she slowed down. She was breathing heavily. She was sweating, and opposite a round bulletin board she stopped. She leaned against the pillar with the notices stuck on it, took a handkerchief out of her bag, and wiped her forehead.

An army jeep drove down the street. The jeep stopped next to her, and she began running again. On Ben Yahuda Street she slowed down. Her hair was disheveled and it seemed to her that her mascara was smudged too. She had a little mirror in her bag, but she was afraid to stand under a streetlight to look in it. She wanted to go into a cafe, but she was drawn toward Mograbi instead. She looked at the advertisements for the movie that was playing at the cinema. The box office was closed. A young boy with red hair was sitting on the railing outside the box office. She looked at him, and he jumped down and said: "You want tickets?"

She didn't take in what he said.

"Come on," he said. "If you want tickets, it's over here, in the corner."

She stayed where she was.

"I'll show you," he said and started walking away.

She followed him. They crossed an open courtyard and entered a basement lit by a number of oil lamps. Two men with their collars open and their ties loosened around their necks were selling tickets. "It's here," said the boy and walked off. The walls of the basement were unpainted and through the thin plaster the outlines of the bricks were visible. She had a five lira note in her hand. Someone pushed a ticket into her hand, took the money with rough fingers, and dropped the change into her open palm. She went on standing next to the door, counted the change, and stared at the oil lamps which were standing on a row of wooden boxes stacked against the wall.

She returned to the Mograbi steps, climbed up to the glass doors, and gave her ticket to the doorman. Then she went down to the bathrooms, combed her hair, and put fresh mascara on her eyelashes. She discovered a stain on her dress. She wet the place with water, rubbed it, and waited. The wet spot dried, but the stain was still there.

When she entered the hall it seemed to her that everyone could see the stain on her dress. She hid it with her bag, and kept her bag over it until she found her place at the end of a row, next to the wall, and sat down. She didn't pay any attention to the woman sitting next to her. She didn't pay any particular attention to the movie either, which seemed to her to go on forever. The colors danced in front of her eyes, her head ached. Little by little she settled down and forgot that she was far from home, in a strange movie theater, by herself. When the movie ended she felt her strength returning, and she turned again in the direction of the promenade. A strong wind was blowing from the sea, and people were leaving the sidewalks, going into cafes, restaurants, gaming alleys. Next to one of the upended barrels she saw a group of soldiers. "Place your bets!" the voice of the man in charge of the game rose above the wind. She approached. "Hey, you!" she heard the skinny man calling as he shook the dice. "Put your money down! Put down a lira! Put down five! Put your money down!"

She skirted the group of soldiers crowding around the barrel. She saw a man come running out of the cafe behind them, and averted her eyes and looked at the soldiers. From behind they looked exactly alike. It was hard for her to distinguish among them. The man who had emerged from the restaurant pushed his way through the people crowding under the awning. When he came face-to-face with her he stood stock-still.

"Hagar," he cried, "Hagar, what are you doing here?"

She stepped back. She didn't say a word. Opposite her, in a pressed suit and tousled hair, stood Noah Bulkin.

12

The main street was dark and deserted. The streetlights had already gone out, and a dull gleam rose from the black asphalt and spread over the sidewalks. The headlights of the cab shone on the road and wiped away the shadows of the trees lining the avenue. The noise of the motor was barely audible, and the car seemed to be gliding, sliding down the road of its own accord. The cab drove around the square and stopped next to the sidewalk opposite Kasos's cafe.

When the cab stopped its lights went off. The door opened, and a woman stepped out.

"Aren't you afraid of walking home by yourself?" asked the cabdriver.

"No. Thank you," replied the woman.

She straightened her dress and began walking along the sidewalk. The headlights of the cab, which had come on again, lit up her figure. Then a dull roar interrupted the silence of the night and the cab backed away. The beams of light retreated too, and the woman walking in them looked as if she were walking to the end of the light and then stepping outside it.

When she emerged from the ficus avenue she turned into a narrow path winding between two wooden fences which led to her house. There was a pale light shining on the corner of the street, but the rest of the houses were already dark and sleeping. Between the slats of her kitchen shutters thin strips of light flickered. The narrow iron gate was closed and wet with dew. She opened the gate carefully and for fear of the unoiled hinges creaking she did not shut it. A cold gust of wind hit her as she entered the yard and tiptoed across the stone path. Splinters of light from the electric bulb in the kitchen penetrated the slits in the shutter.

She was afraid that the door would be locked from inside. She didn't want to knock and wake him up. In her parents' home everyone had a key. Here they only had one key between them. Had he left the key on the windowsill for her? She did that sometimes, when he came back late from Yoel's place. She would open the window and the shutter, stick her hand out, and put the key under the tin can.

She didn't try the door. She went straight to the window, stood on tiptoe, raised her hand to the tin can, and felt the cold stone. The key wasn't there.

She wanted to sleep. A dull, unthinking tiredness filled her. Her eyes burned and she strained to keep them open. She wanted to sit down on the step for a moment and rest, but her feet hurried up the steps and her hand pressed down quickly on the door handle. The door opened with a creak. The light in the kitchen struck her in the face. Quietly she closed the door behind her.

The wine bottle was open on the marble counter. A glass of water next to it. She put her bag down on the table and sat down. Her head dropped, and she held it up with her hands. She closed her eyes and tried to empty herself, as if passing for a moment into another world. It seemed to her that she fell asleep, but she was very aware of her hands pressing on her forehead. She opened her eyes, looked at the wall opposite, at the open window and the closed shutter. Then she spread her hands on the table. Her arms were bare, and a breath of cold air from the window brushed them. Her fingers touched a dry piece of paper. It was the theater ticket which Tuvia had left on the table before going to bed. The stub was still attached to the ticket.

The unused theater ticket woke her up. She snatched it up and examined it for a moment and put it in her bag. Then she stood up, went to the sink, and poured herself a glass of cold water. She took two sips, put the glass down on the counter, and returned to the table. The table was now empty. The ticket was in her bag. She picked up the bag and went to the bathroom. Outside the door she stopped. She returned to the kitchen table, took out the ticket and read everything written on it: the date, hall, price, taxes. She turned it over and tore off the stub. Then she tore the ticket into shreds, and quickly, with big, noisy steps, went back to the bathroom. She shut the door and again she slowed down and walked on tiptoe.

Opposite the mirror she felt very tired again.

She changed her dress for a robe, washed her face, and as she was drying it she saw the swimsuits hanging on the windowsill. Underneath them, in the corner, lay the yellow cloth in which she had wrapped the canteen. She fingered the swimsuits. Tuvia's was already dry. Hers was still damp. She took Tuvia's suit off the window, folded it and put it away in the cupboard. She was now wearing her robe and slippers. She put her shoes on the rack and threw her stockings into the laundry basket. All that was left was the canteen wrapped in the yellow dishcloth.

She took it with her back to the kitchen. Then she went into the living room, switched on the light, and removed the glasses from the table. She cleaned the table, tidied it, switched off the light, returned to the kitchen sink and washed the dishes. There were dry breadcrumbs scattered on the floor and she took a broom, swept them up, and threw them into the trash can. The torn theater ticket was now in her robe pocket. She took the scraps out of her pocket and threw them too into the trash.

The bedsprings creaked. It seemed to her that Tuvia had woken up, and she froze in place. But the creaking stopped, and no more sounds came from the bedroom, not even the sound of Tuvia's breathing. A rustle of dry leaves and branches came from outside the window.

In the corner of the hall stood the sewing machine, covered with a white, embroidered cloth. In the electric light filtering in from the kitchen she went up to the machine, lifted the cloth a little and quietly opened the drawers. She took out thread, needles, a tape measure and a pair of scissors, and returned to the kitchen.

In the kitchen she sat down at the table, took the canteen and the dishcloth, measured, cut and pinned the cloth. She was absorbed in her work and forgot that it was late at night. The noise made by the snipping of the scissors didn't bother her either. She was thirsty, and before sewing the sides of the cloth together, she filled the kettle and put it on the gas. The kettle was heavy. There was a thick layer of kettle-scale at the bottom. "I should clean it soon," she said to herself. She made tea, squeezed lemon juice into it, and returned to the table. She left an opening in the cover and sewed buttons onto it so that Yiftach would be able to slip the canteen in and out. And so that he would be able to attach it to his belt she took a strip of cloth and made it into a loop. When she was finished sewing she put the canteen into the cover, fastened the buttons, and snipped off the black threads sticking out of the seams.

She stood in the dark hall and looked at the clock. The dark hands stood at nearly three o'clock in the morning. She wound the clock and went slowly into the bedroom. Tuvia turned over, and she stood still, hugging the wall.

Her nightgown was lying on top of the white summer coverlet. She bent down, reached out, and pulled it toward her. Standing next to the wall she put it on. She folded her robe and put it on the bedside cupboard.

When she approached the bed and lifted the covers, the wind beat against the shutter. It seemed to her that Tuvia was awake, underneath the coverlet, watching her silent movements.

She was already under the covers. It was hot. She lay on the edge of the bed, as if she were afraid to get into it, and she almost fell out. She pushed her head into the pillow and tried to fall asleep.

Tomorrow she would give the canteen and the cover to Yiftach. It would be a present in honor of the end of the school year. She remembered that he had wanted to tell her something on the day when they had gone for a walk

in the Arab village and the soldier had given her the canteen. Why hadn't he told her? Her eyes were open and
she turned over and lay on her back. Although Tuvia's
breathing was rhythmic, it seemed to her that he wasn't
sleeping. He turned over again and lay on his back. She
tried to squint in his direction. But from the far side of
the bed she couldn't see anything. If he had asked her
anything now, she wouldn't have known what to say.

The alarm clock ticked next to her. Tuvia lay on the
other side of the bed. If he wasn't sleeping – he was
thinking. Thinking of the questions he wanted to ask her.
She was thinking too. But not of the answers. She was
trying to make out the ceiling. Tuvia too, whether he was
sleeping or not, had his face turned toward the ceiling.
And so they "spoke" between themselves.

She didn't remember when and how she fell asleep.

And in the morning, when the alarm clock went off,
she put out her hand to stop the ringing. She was too
tired to wake up, and when the ringing was silenced she
buried her head in the pillow, under the coverlet, and listened to Tuvia, who threw off the covers, sat up, put on
his slippers, and shuffled to the bathroom. Then she
heard the doors opening, the shutters rising, and the
water splashing. When silence fell in the house and the
roar of his motor died away in the street, she peeped at
the clock. It was five-forty in the morning.

At noon she woke again. She dressed, drank a cup of
coffee, switched on the radio, straightened the house,
and when the sun was in the middle of the sky she took
her bag and went to visit her parents again. There she

had lunch with her mother. Afterward she helped her clear the table, got her books and returned home. The exercise books were dusty and yellowed. The pages of the textbooks were stiff, crumbling, unpleasant to the touch. They smelled of mold, and she asked herself how they could be revived. She left them open on the table and went to the village center. There she bought new exercise books, a pencil, a ruler, and a notebook. On the way home she bought food at Tabak's, and when she walked past Kasos, he gave her a strange look.

At home she wrote a letter applying to take her exams at the end of summer. She stuck a stamp on the envelope and went out to mail it. In the street her eyes were drawn to the ruined Arab village. There were no soldiers there today, but there was a red flag flying on one of the roofs.

The mailbox stood on the corner of the street, where the sand met the asphalt. Children were running about the empty lot, and she looked for Yiftach among them. She wanted to tell him she had already sewn the cover for the canteen. She dropped the letter into the box. Yiftach wasn't there, and she went on walking down the road toward the Arab village. She walked slowly, her hands empty. When she reached the place where Bulkin's empty sacks were usually heaped she stopped. Now she had a clear view of the red flag, and she also heard the sharp explosions of the wooden bullets among the ruined houses. She went into the abandoned field. The donkey grazing in the field had freed itself of its tether and it trotted toward her. There was no one to be seen in the Arab village, and she went home.

She didn't leave the house again, and about an hour later she found herself standing in front of the sink peeling potatoes, chopping vegetables, meat, and fruit. She prepared the evening meal, and while the potatoes were boiling she sat down at the table and tried to study. She had forgotten everything. She opened one of her old exercise books and began copying its contents into a new exercise book. She copied in a firm, clear hand, divided the contents into chapters and paragraphs, underlining the headings with her pencil and ruler.

After copying three pages and turning off the gas, she picked up a book and went to sit on the veranda. Evening was falling, and although there were no clouds in the sky, and the horizon over the rooftops was purple, it was chilly out. The children scattered and went home. The red flag was lowered. In Simcha Strauss's house the lights were already on. Tuvia would be home from work any minute now.

The cool air outside made her shiver, and she went in to fetch a shawl, which she wrapped around her arms. When she heard the noise of the jeep and saw the jet of yellow light touching the sand, she went inside. She collected her books from the table and put them on the dresser, next to the canteen.

The jeep entered the yard. Hagar stared at the tiles above the sink. She waited for him to come in. But he delayed, and she too began moving aimlessly about the kitchen. Only when she heard his steps on the veranda did she turn back to the sink and in a kind of panic begin washing a plate under the tap.

Tuvia opened the door, came inside, went over to the table and said, "Good evening."

"Hello," she said. She wanted to add, "Why didn't you come home for lunch?" but instead she asked: "How do you feel, tired?"

"So-so," he said. "Is there hot water?"

"Yes," she said, "go into the bathroom, I'll bring your clothes."

They didn't touch each other, and he walked with a heavy tread to the bathroom.

In the meantime she laid the table.

"And today of all days you made something special," he said after they began to eat.

"Yes, it was ready for lunch," she lied.

"I thought there was something the matter. I didn't know you'd make lunch."

"I know."

"I'm tired," he said suddenly, "as usual on Sundays. It's hard to get used to work all over again."

"I'm tired too."

"I still have to be at Yoel's for about half an hour. Then I'll come home and we'll go to bed early."

"All right," she said.

And then she added: "You see the books on the dresser. I've begun to study. I sent a letter too, to register for the exams."

"Do you still remember anything?"

"At first I thought I'd forgotten everything. I began to copy the material and it started coming back. I even remember the teacher who lectured to us. He stuttered a little, but he made sense, I think."

"Were they at home, yesterday?"

"No, but I have a key."

"But you went again today, didn't you?"

She said nothing.

"Did we get any mail?" he asked.

"No."

"I'll come home early," he said before he left. And she was left with her books again. It seemed to her that she hadn't been out all day, and the heat in the room made her feel languid. She took an exercise book and a textbook onto the veranda and sat down at the table. It was cool outside. Mosquitoes flew around the bare lightbulb. A mosquito dove from the ceiling and stabbed her arm. She scratched the bite and went on copying. She wrote mechanically, smoothing her hair with her fingers. She felt untidy. She ran out of patience with the exercise books and textbooks. She took a book from the bookcase, but tired of that immediately too. "Have a little patience, a little fortitude," she said to herself. But it didn't help. She couldn't study. She couldn't read. A few solitary lights were dotted over the mountains, on the other side of the border. During the day she saw the mountains as azure blue, as gray. Now they were invisible. The lights seemed to be suspended in the air. Suddenly she wanted Tuvia to be at her side. But before her eyes she saw the stooping soldier limping along the stone wall in the ruined village. She remembered the three soldiers who had looked at her yesterday in Allenby Street. If she had met Yiftach this afternoon, she would have gone to the Arab village with him again. In spite of the red flag. Tomorrow morning she would give him the canteen. What was it he had wanted to tell her that day? She smiled to herself. The mosquitoes buzzed in front of her eyes. The dew sparkled on the bushes in the garden. She wanted to sleep.

But when she heard the jeep coming down the street she opened her exercise books again and went on copying.

"Did you get anything done?" asked Tuvia.

"Not so much," she said.

"I'll read the paper first," he said, "and then we'll go to bed. You can take advantage of the mornings."

"Tomorrow morning I may go to the school, to see the principal."

He changed his shoes for slippers, brought a folding deck chair out onto the veranda, opened it, and lay down on it. The newspaper covered his face. Now she had to copy, but she was still doing it mechanically, without concentrating on the words.

"Do you want something to drink?"

"Yes," he said.

She made cold lemonade, gave it to him, and sat down on the balustrade of the veranda. They drank their lemonade in slow sips. Tuvia let the newspaper slip from his hand and it fell to the floor. They didn't talk. He looked at her. She looked at the table, but she didn't see the exercise books. It was only after setting the empty glass down on the balustrade and hearing its faint click that she rose from her place and returned to the table.

"Should we go to bed?" he stood up and leaned on the table.

"I want to study tonight."

"You've got the whole day," he said. "Does it have to be tonight?"

"I have to start sometime."

"It's a long time since we went to bed, to sleep, together. There's always something."

She didn't answer him and he went to bed, alone.

Later on she returned with her books to the kitchen, opened the shutter, and stood next to the screen looking outside, into the night.

13

The day had already begun to dawn, but the house was still in darkness. A long horn blast rose from the street. The first to wake was his mother, after that his father. In the end he too got out of bed and went to the kitchen in his pajamas. Sarah opened the shutter and looked outside. The blasts were sharper now, and on the path leading to the house she saw Hilmi, Bulkin's Arab. The honking stopped and was replaced by a soft knocking on the door. Sarah went to open it. The knocking too stopped, and only the muffled sound of the motor filled the cold, crisp morning air.

"Good morning all," said Hilmi.

Sarah looked at him in surprise, and the Arab continued: "Is he ready?"

"Who?"

"Yiftach. The two of us are driving to Acre now, to buy horses."

In the meantime Yiftach had dressed, and put on his sandals, and washed his face, and he too was now standing at the door.

Sarah looked at him. "Out of the question," she said. "It's true that his vacation starts today, but he can't spend the whole day wandering around in Acre."

The motor in the street died down. Noah Bulkin joined in the conversation.

"Oh Sarah, Sarah," he said, "what's the matter with you today? In any case you're taking the bus to Dr. Volowitz. Why should Yiftach spend the whole day on his own?"

"I'm leaving him with Hagar. He's not on his own. Where will he eat? In a restaurant?"

Simcha, her husband, did not interfere in the conversation. They saw him going from the bedroom to the bathroom, and then emerging in his work clothes.

"All right," she said suddenly. "He can go. And you, don't dawdle there. Come back early. I want him to eat supper at least at Hagar's. All you get in those restaurants is fat."

They returned to the Morris, and Sarah remained standing on the steps, looking at them. Noah Bulkin was already sitting in the cab when she came up and said: "So at least come inside and have a cup of coffee. Yiftach hasn't had his breakfast yet."

"We've already had coffee," said Bulkin, but Hilmi tugged at his shirt. "Yallah, come on," he said.

When he got down from the cab he saw Tuvia Erlich. He was wiping the dew off the windshield of the jeep where it glittered in the morning light. When he saw Bulkin Tuvia left the rag on the hood, walked up to the fence and called: "How's the Morris, Bulkin?"

Bulkin said nothing. He turned to look at the Morris and seemed to nod. The Morris was gleaming in a fresh coat of green paint. The paint had been roughly applied, and the presence of previous layers of paint under it was evident. Bulkin looked back at Tuvia, and as if remembering his question said: "Okay, the Morris is okay."

Yiftach wolfed his omelet. Bulkin and Hilmi stood behind him drinking the black coffee Sarah had poured for them. Bulkin was wearing narrow, brown, corduroy trousers and an army parka. On his head he had a flat cap. He was shaved and the rose-scented aftershave lotion flooded the kitchen. Hilmi was wearing a khaki shirt and trousers. He was unshaven, but he had a kaffiyeh on his head. Because of the stubble on his cheeks and chin he looked older than Bulkin although he was actually far younger than Noah.

Simcha ate his omelet in silence. "I'll be needing you next week," Noah said to him.

"What for?"

"I want to install electricity in the stable. In the shed."

"Okay," said Simcha, "I can do it for you on Saturday."

"I have to wait until Saturday?" said Bulkin.

"A minute ago you said next week!"

"Yes, but I meant tomorrow."

"We'll see," said Simcha. He looked as if he were still half asleep.

The old Haifa road was completely in shadow. Only high above, in the canopy of the eucalyptus trees, pale sunbeams sailed. It was still chilly, and Bulkin hadn't taken off his parka yet. Yiftach sat between Bulkin and Hilmi, and watched Bulkin's hand changing the gears.

The engine chugged. Hilmi leaned his head against the window and tried to sleep. Bulkin hummed a tune.

"What do you need a horse for?" asked Yiftach.

"A mule, not a horse."

"Okay, a mule. What do you need one for? Now that you've got the Morris, why don't you buy a tractor as well?"

"You've got a head on your shoulders, you know that?" said Bulkin. "But I need a mule. For plowing, and for other little things. Besides, I haven't got the money for a tractor."

"Have you ever been to Acre?" asked Hilmi, suddenly waking up.

"No," said Yiftach.

"If Bulkin agrees, we'll go visit my family too. You'll eat something good. Maybe we'll even go out for a bit with the fishermen, in the sea."

"When has Bulkin ever not agreed?" Bulkin stopped

humming. "Especially when Hilmi's got such a pretty sister."

"*Uskut!*" said Hilmi. "Don't talk about my sister. She's not one of your girls."

"I'm not allowed to say your sister's a piece? I'm not the only one who'd take her."

"You'd never marry her," said Hilmi.

"I'm not what you think I am," said Bulkin.

"That's enough. Don't make jokes about my sister. It isn't healthy," said Hilmi, leaning against the window again and closing his eyes.

It was hot inside the cab, and Bulkin told Yiftach to open the window against which Hilmi was leaning.

"But I can't," said Yiftach.

"So wake him up," said Bulkin. "This isn't a hotel."

"He doesn't have to wake me," said Hilmi, and opened the window himself. A cool wind blew in.

They reached Haifa and drove along the bay. "Before we get down to business I think we should have another cup of coffee," said Hilmi.

"Okay," said Bulkin, "but after business we'll go and visit your sister."

"She'll hide behind the curtain."

Bulkin laughed. Yiftach felt hot.

Crates of vegetables, cages of chickens, baskets of fish. Dirt on the floor, close walls, narrow stone streets, shouts. The market. Stalls selling drinks between the crates and the baskets of fish. Stained rubber aprons on the fishmongers' bellies. Little tables projecting into the street, and people sitting around them eating. A strange smell of the sea, rotten fruit, and papers littering the paving stones of the narrow street. Meat on hooks. Stairs. Children running up and down them, disappearing into dark doorways gaping in the long, blank walls.

The Morris drove slowly among the people, the stalls, the crates, and the shouts.

"Stick close to us all the time," said Bulkin. "I don't want to lose you."

Yiftach was silent. Frightened, he nodded his head to show he understood.

Then Hilmi disappeared.

"Where's he gone?" asked Yiftach.

"We'll meet up later," said Bulkin. "Don't worry, just stick with me."

The horses, mules and donkeys were standing in a big paved yard covered with straw. Temporary tin troughs were lined up along the fence and pails of water were dotted about. Bulkin and Yiftach went in and stopped at the entrance. The traders were grooming the animals, brushing their coats, cleaning out their feet, polishing their hooves. There weren't many buyers. Next to the fence they saw Hilmi between two horse dealers.

"There he is," Yiftach pointed to him.

Bulkin slapped Yiftach's hand. "Quiet," he said. "Don't mention his name now."

There was a man selling nuts and sunflower seeds standing at the gate. Bulkin bought a quarter kilo of pistachio nuts, took a handful out of the bag, and gave the rest to Yiftach: "Eat," he said. "Thank you," said Yiftach.

"And keep your mouth shut." Bulkin spat the shells on the floor.

Not far from the nut vendor, next to a break in the stone wall, lay an old man covered with sacks. Flies and mosquitoes were buzzing around his gray beard, and there was saliva dribbling from the corners of his mouth. Bulkin approached him and threw a few peanuts onto the floor. The peanuts fell next to the old man's head, but he didn't wake up. "Look at that floor rag," said Bulkin to Yiftach.

They wandered around among the horses.

"Have a look at these teeth," an Arab horse dealer called out to Bulkin.

"Gold teeth," said Bulkin. "Thank you very much."

"Big mouth," said the Arab. "Come and look first, and talk later."

Bulkin didn't reply. "He's looking for a mule, not a horse," said Yiftach.

"You, keep quiet." Bulkin cuffed him on the side of the head. "Eat your pistachios and spit the shells out on these cheats and keep your mouth shut."

"Here's Hilmi," said Yiftach.

"Why do you talk so much?" said Bulkin. "You don't know Hilmi, understand?"

Hilmi's shirt was hanging outside his trousers, with a thick, brown belt fastened around it. He held a long stick decorated with stripes black as coal. A thick pipe was stuck between his teeth. He walked round among the mules, hitting them with the stick and puffing on his pipe.

Bulkin and Yiftach approached the mules too. Bulkin went up to one of them, examined its legs, opened its mouth, and felt its white teeth with his fingers.

"It only arrived yesterday from Cyprus," said the dealer, a short man wearing a suit and a stained tie.

"The day before yesterday," said Bulkin, and glanced at Hilmi, who pointed with his stick at a young mule standing next to the fence. It was a brown mule, with a black stripe running all the way down its back to its long tail, which swept the floor. A bespectacled dealer ran his hand over the black stripe.

Next to the bespectacled horse dealer stood another one with a gray mule dappled with black.

Hilmi stood next to the brown mule and spoke to the dealer.

Bulkin went up to the gray mule with Yiftach.

"Don't say anything to anyone," said Bulkin. "Keep your mouth shut." They went right up to the gray mule, and Bulkin began feeling it.

"Good merchandise," said the dealer. "It only got off the ship from Cyprus yesterday."

"Let's have a look," said Bulkin.

"Only five hundred," Bulkin heard the second dealer haggling with Hilmi.

"Only five hundred," Bulkin's dealer echoed.

Bulkin felt the gray mule's back, but his eyes were on the brown mule over which Hilmi was bargaining with the bespectacled dealer. The dealer's eyes looked tiny behind his thick glasses. He was thin and his two front teeth were missing. His hair was combed back and he was wearing gray trousers and a striped shirt. His voice was hoarse and squeaky.

"I'll take it for four hundred," said Hilmi. He lifted the mule's tail, and stroked the long hair falling to the ground like a quiet stream, he felt its legs. The mule's brown eyes were big and watering and mosquitoes clustered at their corners.

"Four hundred? Are you crazy?" said the dealer. "This is the best merchandise you'll find in the market today. "

"Look," said Hilmi, "a mule isn't a machine. Today you can buy a car for five hundred."

"Tell me, where did you spring from?" said the dealer. And when he saw that Hilmi was still hanging around the mule he added: "Get away from this mule."

"We haven't finished yet," Hilmi persisted. "I want this mule. But not for five hundred. It's not worth it. Look," and he pointed to the mule next to which Bulkin was standing, "for that black one they want five hundred, and for this nag you want five hundred too? You can have my hand before I'll give you five hundred for this carcass."

"Carcass?" yelled the dealer. "You're a carcass yourself, you dirty Arab. Bugger off. Yesterday it got off the ship from Cyprus. Go on, bugger off, dirty Arab. Don't dirty me. Go. I wouldn't give you this mule even for five hundred. Carcass?! Have you ever heard the like?"

"Stop calling me dirty Arab, you hear?" Hilmi left the mule and approached the dealer. "I'm not an Arab and I'm no dirtier than you are. That is, I'm an Arab, but not the way you say it. And you will sell me the mule. This carcass isn't worth five hundred, and you'll sell it to me for what it's worth."

"Bugger off!" yelled the dealer, and advanced on Hilmi who didn't even take the pipe out of his mouth. "Go on, bugger off!" he screamed. "I'll sell the mule to anyone else for two hundred and fifty. But not to you, not even if you gave me a thousand. . . ."

"For two hundred and fifty?" asked a quiet voice. Bulkin's voice.

"For a lira!" yelled the dealer. "Only not to that dirty Arab!"

Bulkin's wallet was already open, and he pushed three hundred lira into the dealer's outstretched hand. "It's a deal," he said quietly.

"Untether the mule, hurry up." He turned to Yiftach, who hurried to the post and untied the reins.

The bespectacled dealer counted the money, and looked at Bulkin. "What's this? Three hundred! Who are you? Where's that cheeky Arab?"

Hilmi had already vanished among the horses and people filling the yard, and Yiftach followed him, pulling the brown mule with the black stripe behind him.

"You won't get more," said Bulkin. "It's a nice mule, I grant you, but it's not worth more." He shook the dealer's hand, said "Thanks," and walked away.

"Crooks!" the trader flung after Bulkin, but he could no longer see him.

When he passed the ragged old man lying next to the hole in the wall, Bulkin stopped for a moment. The handful of peanuts he had thrown onto the paving stones was gone.

"What a sly fox!" said Bulkin to himself, and he threw another handful of peanuts to the old man.

Bulkin reached the Morris and helped Hilmi load the mule into the back of the van.

"Now we have to cut the tail," said Hilmi.

"We'll do it at your sister's," said Bulkin. "In any case it's a good thing you're an Arab. Otherwise I would have paid five hundred."

Hilmi seated Yiftach on his lap, and they drove slowly down the narrow street, between the people, the crates, and over the little cobblestones on the street. Yiftach looked through the back window of the cab and saw the mule's brown, watering eyes.

"Look ahead," said Bulkin, "at the road. You'll have plenty of time to look at the horse later. So, did you see something today? In life the thing is to keep a man to his word."

Yiftach turned around, and looked at the road in front of them. "It isn't a horse, "he said quietly. "It's a mule."

They had lunch at Hilmi's family home. His sister prepared a drink from rosewater, and his father took the mule behind the house, and cut its mane and bobbed its tail.

"She's pretty, your sister," said Bulkin when they were on their way home.

Hilmi was silent. And Yiftach, who could still taste the roses on his lips, said: "If I knew we were going to drink that rosewater I would have brought my canteen."

"You've got a canteen?"

"Yes," he said. "A soldier gave it to me. But Hagar is making me a bag for it now, and she took the canteen home with her."

"She likes roaming around too much, that Hagar," said Hilmi.

"But she's pretty," said Bulkin. "Almost as pretty as your sister."

14

"I'll be back early today," Sarah said to her, "but if I'm late, give Yiftach supper. He went off to Acre today with that Bulkin and his Arab. Maybe it's for the best. I've decided to put the baby into an institution. Dr. Volowitz is right. I'm just being stubborn."

They were standing in Hagar's yard, on the garden path, next to the empty mailbox. Sarah was ready to leave, and Hagar didn't know what to say. But suddenly she blurted out: "Would you like me to come with you? Perhaps you'll need help?"

"There's no need," said Sarah. "Thank you very much. I don't know what I'd do without you. Perhaps I will come back late. Or even tomorrow. I'll want to see how they look after him in the home." She sighed and looked down at the path. "Look after Yiftach for me," she said then in a quiet voice. "I shouldn't have sent him off with Bulkin. I don't know what's gotten into him lately. He's not happy," said Sarah. "He doesn't play with the other children."

"He's a wonderful boy," said Hagar. "Believe me."

Sarah walked off. "If they come back early," Hagar called after her, "I'll go for a walk with him in the Arab village." But Sarah was already on the other side of the road, and Hagar went inside. On the dresser she saw the canteen. She took it and went outside. She ran lightly across the dirt road and went into the Strauss's yard. Sarah was already standing on the doorstep with the baby in her arms. She had a black scarf tied around her hair and the dark lines on her unmade-up face stood out in the sunlight.

"I forgot something," said Hagar. "I promised Yiftach to make him a cover for the canteen. Here it is," she held the canteen out to Sarah. "Why don't we leave it here in the house for him and give him a surprise."

Sarah stepped down from the door. "Go in and leave it on the table," she said to Hagar.

Afterward Hagar accompanied Sarah on her way. "Is it from the soldiers?" asked Sarah.

"Yes, I found it. But they didn't want it back. One of the soldiers gave it to Yiftach for a present."

"I envy you," said Sarah, "for having the time to go for walks. When I come back from Dr. Volowitz I hope I'll have more time to devote to Yiftach. I'll go for walks with him too. That Arab village is a wonderful place. I remember it from the time when they still lived there.

We used to buy eggs there, and goat's milk." Sarah spoke calmly, as if she weren't carrying the blind baby in her arms.

That day again Tuvia didn't come home for lunch, and Hagar once more received a curious look from Kasos on her way back from Tabak's grocery store. Tabak's wife hardly spoke to her either, and when she returned her change she didn't even greet her but asked right away: "Who's next in line?" But this time Hagar stared back at Kasos and went up to him. She bought a glass of juice, and asked: "Did he have lunch here again today?"

Kasos was embarrassed. He wiped his hands on his apron, took off his hat, exposing the bald spot in the middle of his head, and said quietly: "Yes, he did."

Hagar finished the juice and before leaving she said: "Then at least cook him a decent meal, not the same as you give everyone else."

Kasos advanced to the entrance, leaned against the doorjamb, and said, "You come with him one day. I'm a good cook. But everyone gets the same." He spoke loudly now, but he didn't see Hagar's narrow lips and her green eyes fixed on the floor in inexplicable bitterness.

She didn't go to the school or open a book the whole day long. She put the groceries she had bought at Tabak's away in the cupboard and the refrigerator. She didn't cook, and for her lunch she had two apples and a cup of coffee. She tried to take a nap in the afternoon, but when she didn't fall asleep she kept getting up to look through the kitchen window at Yiftach's house. She wanted to know if he were back. But the shutters were closed. and the yard was empty except for one big sheet hanging on the laundry line.

The street was deserted too, the sand blazed in the heat. Even the children were hiding inside their houses or in the shade of the Pride of India trees in their yards. Nevertheless Hagar went out, with a textbook in her knitting bag. She went to the Arab village. Through the orange groves, along the path passing Bulkin's yard. She was wearing sandals, and occasionally she stumbled against a hummock of blazing sand that burned her bare feet. A hot buzz of mosquitoes rose from the grove, and the smell of wilted blossoms struck her nostrils.

Voices came from Bulkin's shed. The Morris was parked in the yard. A brown mule, its tail bobbed, was tethered to the electric pole. It was eating hay from a broad wooden box. Next to the box stood a pail of water. It was a young mule and it seemed to her that its eyes, in spite of the tears and the flies that filled them, were gazing at her. She went into the yard and walked toward the voices.

In front of the door to Bulkin's house, next to the can of glue and the red posters, lay a torn sack stained with dry mud. Bulkin's black boots lay next to the dripping tap.

Chips of wood, rusty nails and screws came flying out of the shed window into the yard. The window was caked with dust, and the nails seemed to be falling out of a dry, heavy fog.

"Here's Hagar," called Hilmi to Bulkin. He came out and took up the rake leaning against the shed wall.

"Hello," said Hagar. "You're back already?"

"Can't you see the merchandise we brought back with us?" said Bulkin, emerging from the shed. His head was covered with dust, and he slapped his hands against his trousers to shake off the bits of straw and dirt sticking to them.

"That donkey?" said Hagar.

"That mule," said Bulkin. "Look at his tail, at the way Hilmi's father docked it for him. You call that a donkey? He's not even a mule. He's a prince." He went to the tap and washed his hands, and then he held out his hand to Hagar.

Hagar transferred the knitting bag to her left hand and gave him her right hand. "Where's Yiftach?" she asked.

"What's your hurry?" said Bulkin. "Come in and have a cup of coffee. His voice was lower now, and slightly hesitant. It seemed to Hagar that he was blinking.

"Thank you," said Hagar, and smiled. "I've just had some."

"You don't drink coffee because you're thirsty," said Bulkin. "We brought pistachio nuts from Acre too."

"And where's Yiftach?"

"He went down to the center," said Hilmi, who had been leaning on the handle of the rake all this time and rocking to and fro on it, as if he were praying. "I think he went to your place, to get the canteen. But he said he'd come back here."

"But the canteen's not there now, and there's nobody at home. I have to go," she said quickly. And when she was already at the gate she called: "Thanks for the coffee. Another time."

Hilmi ran behind her, caught up with her, and opened the gate for her.

Hagar hurried home. She thought she might meet Yiftach in time to take him for a walk, as she had promised Sarah. But the road was deserted and their gate was shut. There was no sign that anyone had opened it. She went into Sarah's yard. The laundry was still on the line, but the gate was open. The door to the house, however, was shut, and nobody answered her knock. She tried to peep inside, to see if Yiftach were there, but all the shutters were closed, and it was impossible to see anything through the slats, except for darkness.

She knew where to look for him. There was nobody in the empty lot yet. She walked toward the Arab village, taking the path through the orange groves again, past Bulkin's land. But this time she didn't cut across Bulkin's place. She didn't want to bump into Noah and his Arab. She walked along a narrow path leading through the orange grove and peeped through the trees into Bulkin's yard. The Arab was standing next to the electric pole. He untethered the mule and led it to the shed which had been converted into a stable. Bulkin was standing next to the tap and reading one of the posters lying on the ground. Yiftach wasn't there.

She stepped off the path, and walked through the trees. Dry leaves crumbled under her sandals, a stifling smell rose into the air together with clouds of mosquitoes. The branches scratched her arms and she walked faster. When she emerged into the field she breathed a sigh of relief, in spite of the glare of the sun.

There was no red flag over the village now. Nor was there any smoke rising from the houses. She couldn't see a single soldier. A truck passed on the road. In the distance, between the hills, lay a heavy, yellow haze. Was Yiftach somewhere in the village? She decided to go and look.

The shadow of a man flitted across one of the ruined walls. Stones tumbled down with a loud clatter. She felt nervous about going on toward the houses and stopped at the olive trees. She sat down on the stones, put down the knitting bag, and looked around. When she heard nothing, she took out her work and began to knit.

"Hi, you there," she heard a cry ring out.

She looked behind her, but there was no one there. She stood up and walked slowly toward the first ruined house of the village. A rough, broken shadow crossed the wall. Again she heard stones clattering and footsteps pounding on the sand.

"Yiftach," she called, "Yiftach, stop scaring me. Come here."

"Don't want to." The broken shadow vanished from the wall.

"That's enough. Enough of those games. Come here."

"I'm coming," said the voice. From a breach in the wall he emerged. In fatigues, but without any equipment. The soldier.

His hair was stuck to his forehead. He took a hesitant step toward her, and then stopped. It looked as if he wanted to say something, for he raised his hand, but then he immediately dropped it again.

Hagar shifted her knitting bag from hand to hand. She too said nothing, and looked at the wall next to which the soldier was standing.

The sun was behind her, so that she saw her still shadow lying on the stones.

A thin haze of mosquitoes emerged from the ruined house and flew between them, and Hagar began to walk along the tumbledown alley between the houses. She didn't say a word, and the soldier walked behind her.

"Where is everybody?" she suddenly asked.

He quickened his pace, caught up with her, and fell into step beside her.

"There's nobody here," he said.

"Aren't you training today?"

"Yes. But not here. We've finished here."

She didn't ask him, "What are you doing here?" Her head was bowed, her eyes were on the stones scattered over the path. She walked slowly, afraid of stumbling, and saw the soldier's broken shadow advancing over the stones beside hers.

There were dead embers lying in the shallow drinking troughs carved out of the paving stones around the well. A bad smell rose from the houses and the dirty sand. They didn't stop there. They walked east. In the field of thorns beyond the village they made out a vague path.

The thorns were high, and sometimes the soldier had to clear the way with his feet, with his hands. He would trample a bush with his boots, turn around and say, "Pass." When the path became clearer and wider, she asked: "Where are we going?"

Next to the rutted road which led to the mountains on the other side of the border, they had to cross a deep ditch. The soldier jumped across and then stretched out his hand to her. She gave him the knitting bag. She too jumped, but she almost slipped back into the ditch. "I've grown heavy," she said, as if to herself.

"Where are we going?" said the soldier. "Behind this abandoned *moshav,* there's a side road that leads to a quiet place. We can go there."

The houses of the *moshav* were white and low. Their red roofs had grown rusty. The windows were boarded up. But some of the windows were open to the wind. The yards were overgrown with dry grass. Dry thorns tangled in the sagging fences. The main road of the *moshav,* too, along which they were walking, was eroded, with deep potholes gaping in the earth.

The first house, next to the road, was not unoccupied. The yard was clean. A goat was nibbling the dry grass in front of the shed, and a big dog was running along the laundry line. But the shutters were closed, and the old watchman who lived there was nowhere to be seen. They walked past this house, and a feeling of loneliness flowed out to them from the empty houses.

"So how did you get here?" she asked.

"There isn't much for us to do now. Next week we're going south. For a month, maybe. And over here we've already finished our training. I asked for permission to leave the camp, and they gave it to me."

"What did you do on Saturday?"

"On Saturday? We had a half day off, in the afternoon."

"And where did you go?"

"What do you do on Saturday? Hang out around Mograbi. On the promenade."

"You were there?"

"Yes. We even went to a movie."

"Where? Mograbi?"

"No. Ben-Yahuda."

The road between the *moshav* houses ran in a wide arc, and when it veered north, they left it. There were green shoots sprouting in the fields which were plowed in dry, old furrows. The soldier was still holding her knitting bag in his hand. At the end of the field was a low avenue of broad cypresses. Two palm trees and a lemon tree were planted among them.

"I have to rest a while," said Hagar, and smiled in embarrassment.

The soldier stopped. His face was turned to the east. To the avenue of cypresses, to the tall palm trees, and the distant mountains looming beyond the treetops.

"Are we going to that avenue?" she asked.

"Not exactly. That's only on the way. But we're not far."

"I've never been here before."

"Neither have I," he said, "except for once. At night. We were coming back from an outdoor training session and we passed here. We stopped to rest in the place where we're going."

They crossed the railway tracks. The dry furrows were behind them now and the ground was hard and smooth. There were grooves made by cart wheels in it.

Hagar suddenly turned to look behind her. The sun dazzled her and she blinked her eyes.

"We've already passed the railway line," she said. "We've gone too far, we're far from the village."

"Not so far," he said. "It's the sun in your eyes that makes things seem far. It's hard to see with the sun in your eyes."

"I haven't seen Yiftach all day," she said.

He laughed. "You know," he said, "I thought he was your son."

"Do I look so old to you?"

"No, but I always saw you with him. Except for yesterday."

"What, you saw me yesterday?"

"No," he said. And then in a weak voice he added: "But I waited for you."

"For me?"

"Yes."

"Where?"

"In the Arab village. They let me leave the camp yesterday too. I thought you'd be there."

She was silent.

"No, I wasn't there yesterday," she said finally.

"And who is Yiftach?"

"A neighbor's son."

"Was he pleased with the canteen?"

"I don't know yet. I made him a cover for it, like you have in the army. But from a yellow cloth. I fixed it so he could attach it to his belt too. He hasn't seen it yet. This morning he went to Acre with Bulkin and his Arab. To buy horses. I left it for him at his house. When he comes home he'll have a surprise. Actually, he's back already, but I couldn't find him. His mother asked me to look after him today too. Poor woman."

"What's the matter?"

"Her second child was born not normal. It looks as if she'll have to leave him in an institution."

"And you," asked the soldier, "you live alone?"

They walked along the cypress avenue, and their shadows impinged on the net of black stripes cast by the branches on the ground. Hagar didn't answer.

The cypress avenue ended in a little orchard surrounded by barren lemon trees and pointed posts. Beyond the orchard was an old tarred road. Next to the road there was a sign which said: "Stop! Frontier ahead!"

"We've already passed the railway line," she said. "Where are you taking me?" She took a step toward him and laid her hand on the knitting bag in his hand.

"Don't be frightened," he said, "it's only a warning. It's another four hundred meters to the border." The sign was yellow, and someone had scribbled on it in white chalk. The letters were red.

The road disappeared into a dense orange grove, and the soldier turned onto a side path leading to a deserted building, two stories high. They climbed the stairs to the flat roof. At the edge of the roof was a little swimming pool. The pool was empty. Rain water had collected in stagnant puddles at the bottom of the pool and the walls were covered with green slime. Purple flowers climbed the walls of the house and crawled onto the roof. Before they went down it seemed to them that they saw a figure walking along the cypress avenue. But a light wind had begun to blow at that hour of the afternoon, and perhaps it was only the wind moving the branches and playing with the shadows on the ground.

They went down to the first floor. Colored tiles peeped through the sand, and dry branches covered the floor. There were some torn sacks lying in a corner with burned red bricks stacked on them. They sat down on the bricks.

"I'm tired," said Hagar. She was leaning against the wall and closed her eyes.

The soldier didn't reply. He examined the creases on her forehead. Her skin was pale. Her smooth hair fell onto her forehead and shaded her cheeks and cracked lips. He put the knitting bag down on the sacks, straightened up, and Hagar put her arms around his fatigue shirt, dropped her head onto his shoulder, and wept.

A bird perched on the frameless, shutterless window. It pecked at the stones with its beak, and then flew outside to the trees.

"I haven't got any more strength left," she said suddenly. Her eyes were dry now, and there were only two dark streaks, also dry, running down her cheeks.

The room was stifling. They lay naked on her dress, which was spread over the sacks. Hagar lay on her back, with her head turned toward the pile of his clothes. His black boots were lying opposite her eyes. She reached out her hand and stroked the hard, rough leather.

"I'm cold," he said suddenly.

It seemed to her that she heard a stone clattering among the trees. She took his sweaty shirt which was lying on the floor, shook it out, and spread it over his back.

The noise in the orange grove increased. Branches crashed into each other. Birds clustered opposite the window. Muffled thuds hit the ground.

The soldier entered her. Hagar stroked the veins bulging on his neck, opened her eyes – and listened.

15

Bulkin and Hilmi put Yiftach down in the village square, next to the tall concrete pillar, where the first one to see him was Kasos: "Did they get something worth paying for?" he asked. Yiftach, his tiredness showing in his eyes, said seriously: "A good mule, but they're sly, those two."

Kasos, surprised by the expression, joked: "*Nu*, what do you want? Bulkin is Bulkin."

He had a few pennies in pocket which his mother had given him in the morning, and he bought a glass of soda.

Then he went to his father, but the shop was shut. His father had gone to one of his customer's houses.

He remembered that his mother had asked him to buy two bottles of milk at Tabak's, and before going home he went into the grocery store and bought them on credit.

As he approached his house he saw Tzemach climbing the eucalyptus on the lot and he began to run. He opened the gate, took the key out of his pocket, opened the door, and put the milk bottles down on the table.

Right next to the canteen in the yellow cover which Hagar had made for it.

He left the bottles on the table, picked the canteen up, took it out of its cover and put it back in again. He fingered the yellow cloth and felt the loop. "For the belt," he said to himself. He went to his parents' wardrobe, took out his father's thick leather belt, and tried to put it on. The belt was too big for him. He looked for another belt, but he couldn't find one.

With the belt in his hand, he put the bottles of milk in the refrigerator. Then he went to the tool shed and rummaged among his father's tools. He found an old scissors, a chisel and a hammer. He measured the belt around his waist, made a mark with the chisel, and began to cut. The scissors were blunt, and he beat the leather with the chisel and the hammer. Gradually the belt was severed.

With the help of a screwdriver he made new holes in it and put it on.

Back in the house, he attached the canteen-cover to the belt by the loop and went to the sink to fill the canteen. He took a few sips, corked it, and went to the mirror to inspect himself. Then he opened the shutter and looked across at Hagar's house. All the shutters in her house were closed.

"Maybe she's sleeping," he said to himself, and wearing the wide belt, with the canteen bumping against his thigh, he crossed the street, entered Hagar's yard, walked around the house and knocked on the kitchen door. When there was no reply, he climbed down the steps and raised his eyes to the little can on the windowsill. He looked round. The trees hid him, no one could see. He overturned the pail standing next to the wall, climbed onto it, and held onto the windowsill. The key was there. Hagar wasn't at home.

He didn't know where to find her, and before going to the Arab village he decided to go to Bulkin's place to show him the canteen. He didn't see the mule in the yard, and Hilmi, who was raking around the trees, asked him: "Are you looking for the mule?"

"I brought something to show you," said Yiftach.

"Come and see," said Hilmi.

Hilmi led Yiftach to the shed and opened the tin door. In the darkness Yiftach made out the shape of the mule. They went in, and Yiftach saw the wide trough they had prepared next to the wall, and the big water basin, with the special tap they had installed dripping into it and making sure that the basin was always full.

"All that's missing is electricity," said a coarse voice behind them. It was Bulkin, who had entered the new stable behind Hilmi and Yiftach.

"I'll tell my dad to come soon," said Yiftach.

They went out into the yard, and sat down, all three of them, on the doorstep of Bulkin's house.

"Here's the canteen." Yiftach undid his belt and handed it to Bulkin.

Bulkin opened the canteen, took a sip of water, and handed it to Hilmi. While Hilmi drank, Bulkin inspected the yellow jacket. "Nice work," he said. "Did Hagar make it for you?"

"Yes," said Yiftach.

"So you met her?" asked Bulkin.

"No." This was Hilmi speaking.

"How do you know he didn't?" said Bulkin. "And how did he get the canteen?"

"After she was here, " said Hilmi, "she came back. You've got no eyes. But I saw her. She was walking on the path in the orange grove, and from there she peeked into the yard, to see if Yiftach was here. She didn't want you to go on nagging her with your coffee. Yiftach wasn't here, so she went on to the Arab village, as usual."

Yiftach put the canteen back into its cover and fastened his father's belt.

Hilmi brought up a box from the fence, turned it over, and sat on it. Yiftach undid the buckle of the belt and put the canteen on his lap. They sat in the shade, and Hilmi said suddenly: "We've done enough for today. I think I'm going home."

"Just like that you're leaving me alone?"

"Not alone," Hilmi got up from the box. "With the mule."

Yiftach laughed. "I'm going too," he said.

"Where to?" asked Bulkin.

"To find Hagar."

"Go to the Arab village. She's always hanging around there, looking for something." Hilmi left. He disappeared up the road, behind the cypresses.

"Run along then," said Bulkin to Yiftach. "I've still got things to do today."

Yiftach buckled his belt and walked toward the ruins. He didn't see any flag and he made straight for the middle of the village, for the well and the drinking troughs. He bent down and threw a stone into the well. Rings of water spread out to the sides of the well, carrying the slime and dirt with them. He opened the canteen and poured out the water. Then he looked around for the rope and the pail with which the soldiers drew water from the well. He found the rope and pail next to the stone wall, in a patch of thorns, hidden under a rusty piece of tin. He threw the pail into the well, but it floated on the surface of the water and didn't fill up. He tried to float it on its side, and when it failed to fill with water, he pulled it up and put a stone inside it. Now the pail sank into the water and when it was full of water it plunged to the bottom of the well, pulling Yiftach after it.

He wound the rope around his hand, and with all his strength pulled the pail toward him. The pail was heavy, and the rope rubbed against the skin of his hand and hurt it.

But the pail rose from the well, full of water, and Yiftach filled his canteen. The water was cold and he washed his face in it. Then he returned to the stone wall and hid the pail under the metal sheet between the stones and the thorns.

"So that's where they hide it," said a slow, hoarse, slightly trembling voice behind him.

Yiftach started in alarm.

He turned round and saw the old watchman from the *moshav* standing with his dog not far from the well.

"I got hold of a pail and a rope," said the old man. "but ever since the soldiers came everything disappears. Every time they hide it somewhere else. And now you found it. Good, good." He cleared his throat.

"Were the soldiers here today too?" asked Yiftach.

"No," said the old man, "only one."

"Have you seen Hagar?" asked Yiftach.

"Tuvia's wife?"

"Yes, she made me the cover for this canteen, see?" And he put his hand on the full canteen, whose yellow jacket was wet.

"They passed through the *moshav*. I heard them. Maybe they went on as far as the palms, I don't know. But don't you go there, it's dangerous close to the border. They'll be back soon."

The old watchman left. He crossed the stone wall, and turned toward the village.

Yiftach waited next to the well until the old man vanished from sight, and then he crossed over the ruins of the Arab village, entered the thorn field, and reached the road which ran past the abandoned *moshav*.

He wanted to go into the deserted *moshav,* but as he turned onto the dirt track which ran through its center, his eyes fell on a black spot in the distance. Further along the road, where it curved sharply and the white dome of a sheik's tomb stood out among the eucalyptus trees, he saw Hilmi. "If he's going home," he thought, "he's taking a long way around."

Then he entered the *moshav* and walked toward the avenue of cypress trees.

Again the branches in the orange grove rustled, and through the open, frameless window, she saw a flock of pigeons flying up to the sky.

"Should we get dressed? " she asked.

Hagar was lying with her eyes open, her eyes fixed on the windowsill. She felt cold and she pulled the soldier to her. The shirt covering them fell off.

She heard a creak, something rubbing against the wall, and she saw fingers rising above the windowsill, clinging to the stones of the sill.

She couldn't speak. She looked at the soldier's hair. His head was cradled in her hands, buried in her soft breasts.

The fingers had already invaded the room. They were

small and bunched, and gripped the inner edge of the windowsill. Then she saw the head coming up.

"Yiftach," she wanted to call. But he suddenly let go of the window and his head disappeared. There was the sound of a dull thud on the ground, a rustle of running footsteps and branches colliding with each other.

Her eyes were remote now. The soldier sat up, took his shirt and put it on.

"What's wrong?" He looked at her.

She gave him his shoes and socks and then she too got dressed.

"What's wrong with you?" he asked again as they left the building.

But Hagar only gripped his arm for a moment, said good-bye, and ran away.

The soldier stood next to the yellow frontier sign, and watched her vanishing among the white *moshav* houses.

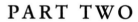

PART TWO

16

"He was looking for you," said the old *moshav* watchman.

Hagar met him on the main road, at the entrance to the *moshav*. His dog sidled up to her legs and sniffed her dress.

It was only after he had repeated himself that she asked, "Who?"

"The boy. Did you meet him?"

"No," she said.

She smoothed her hair down with her fingers and arrived home by a side street. The key was in its place under the can, on the windowsill. She went into the bathroom, washed her face, combed her hair, put her hand on her cheek and felt the warmth of her skin. She took off her clothes. Her dress was creased, and there was a stain from the damp ground on it. She threw the dress into the laundry basket, turned on the hot water tap in the bath.

While the water ran into the tub, she soaked her bra and panties in the sink and washed them with laundry powder. She wrung them out and hung them on the line beside the window. She wanted to put on a robe, to go to the bedroom and fetch herself clean clothes, but the bath was already full and she got in. The water was hot and her teeth chattered, as if with cold. She turned on the cold water tap and picked up the soap.

The window was closed and the room was full of steam. After shampooing her hair she stepped out of the bath and dried herself. She wiped the floor dry with a floor rag, put on her robe, and went into the bedroom and opened the shutters. The roofs of the houses were touched by a violet light. A wind blew into the room and she felt chilled. She got into bed, covered her head with the blanket, relaxed her muscles and fell asleep.

It was already night in the room when she heard some-one knocking at the door.

"Who's there?" she asked, went to the kitchen, and opened the door.

"Good evening."

"Oh, Sarah, Sarah, it's good you came," said Hagar.

Sarah remained standing outside, on the dark veranda. Hagar stretched out her hand to her: "Come in, come in. I was sleeping. I don't know what came over me. Come in, we'll have coffee."

"Have you seen Yiftach?" asked Sarah.

Hagar appeared not to hear the question, and she said:

"You'll have coffee, won't you?"

"Yes," said Sarah.

Sarah sat next to the wall, her elbows leaning on the table. Her eyes were red, and her short hair was threaded with gray. She was wearing a black dress strewn with white flowers, and there were streaks of dried sweat on her neck.

Hagar sat opposite her.

Sarah put a cube of sugar into her coffee, and while she stirred it she asked again: "Where's Yiftach? Have you seen him today?" There were veins standing out on the back of her hand and her nails were carelessly cut.

"Yes, I saw him," said Hagar. Her eyes were fixed on the black coffee. "Would you like a little milk?"

"No, thank you," said Sarah. "I prefer black coffee."

"When did you get back?"

"Just now," she sighed. "That's it. I arranged it with the doctor. He's putting the baby in a home. There's nothing more to be done for him. I wanted to go there today. But the doctor said I should wait. I'll go next week." The steam rising from the coffee covered her face. "I'll have a little more time for Yiftach now," she said. "I've neglected him a bit. Sometimes I look at him and think that although he's only ten years old he's not a child at all. He sits in the kitchen, makes himself an omelet, and eats it slowly, staring at the wall or at Simcha's newspaper."

Hagar went over to the window and looked out through the screen.

"Isn't your husband back from work yet?" she asked Sarah.

"No, he always comes late. But I'm worried about Yiftach not being back yet."

"Perhaps he's at Bulkin's?"

"No, he isn't there. When I got back I met Bulkin. He was sitting in Kasos's cafe. He'd already changed into clean clothes." The coffee cup was empty, but her hand was still gripping it. "He's a lonely man, Bulkin," she murmured to herself.

"He's a bit crude, in my opinion," said Hagar, and she went to the window again and looked outside.

Sarah rose from her place, and before she left she looked at Hagar. "I'm worried," she said. Hagar's lashes were streaked with sleep and her eyes darted round the room.

Sarah closed the door behind her, and Hagar went to the bedroom to fetch her knitting bag. It wasn't there.

"How can I go back there?" she asked herself, returning to the bedroom and throwing herself onto the bed. There was a sound of footsteps on the path. "They won't leave me in peace today," she said to herself and waited for the knock at the door. There were tears in her eyes.

But nobody knocked at the door. The footsteps were heavy and Hagar recognized them. The door opened and Tuvia came into the house.

She wiped her face on the sheet and went into the kitchen.

"Where's the jeep?" she asked.

"Broken down. I left it at the garage."

"And how did you come home?"

"With Yoel." He sat down at the table, where the empty coffee cups were still standing.

"Was someone here?" He took a cookie from the dish.

"Yes. Sarah. Yiftach hasn't come home yet."

"I saw him this morning. Bulkin took him to Acre in the Morris."

She took the cups to the sink and washed them. Mosquitoes droned against the screen, trying to get into the kitchen. She left the sink and went up to the window. She hit the screen with her hand, but the mosquitoes stayed stuck to the fine wire netting. There was no one in the street.

"Hagar, is anything the matter?"

His hand was on her shoulder.

Hagar froze in place. She didn't answer him. Their heads were close to the wire screen and the mosquitoes.

Suddenly she broke away from him and ran out of the kitchen. She went back to the bedroom. Tuvia followed her.

"What's the matter with you?" he said. The room was dark, and he went up to Hagar who was curled up on the corner of the bed. It seemed to him that she was crying, but he grabbed her by the shoulders. "Answer me when I talk to you. Do you hear, answer me, what's the matter with you lately? It's impossible to talk to you. Answer me."

She withdrew into herself, she tried to escape from his hands which held onto her tightly and wouldn't let go. "Tell me," he said, "tell me. Things can't go on like this."

"Don't yell at me," she cried and pushed him away.

In his work clothes he sat down on the bed, on the white coverlet. He let her go and rested his hands on his knees.

From the kitchen came the sound of water boiling and food cooking. He stood up and went to the kitchen and switched off the gas. Dense steam covered the window, hiding the mosquitoes. He stood next to the sink. The steam got into his eyes. His shoes felt heavy and his socks were sticky with sweat. He sneezed, went back to the bedroom, and put his hand on Hagar's shoulder. Her head was on the pillow. Her shoulders shook.

"Do you want something to drink?" he asked.

Hagar stretched out her hand to his knee. The material of his trousers was coarse. His leg trembled.

He couldn't control the trembling of his leg, and he took her hand between his.

She sat up and embraced him. "I feel so bad," she said.

"Rest," he said. "I'll see to the food. You can have supper in bed."

She freed her hand and stretched out on the bed. Tuvia left the room. There was hot water in the kettle, and he made a cup of tea. Then he returned to the bedroom, carrying the cup in one hand and dragging a chair in the other. He switched on the light, pulled the chair up to the bed, and put the cup on it. Hagar was lying on her back. Her eyes were closed, and he put his hand on her forehead. "Drink," he said. She didn't say anything, or open her eyes, and he went to take a shower.

When she heard the water running in the shower, she sipped the tea, got up, and went back to the kitchen. She raised the lid of the saucepan. A smell of burned potatoes overwhelmed her. Her head ached. She drank a glass of cold water, got a fork, and examined the potatoes. The burned ones she threw into the trash, but when she tasted the good ones, she discovered that they had a burned taste too.

While she was laying the table she suddenly felt weak at the knees. She sat down and waited. Her arms rested on the smooth table from which she had removed the cloth, and a delicate coolness caressed her skin.

After the meal Tuvia cleared the table and washed the dishes. They went to bed. It was nine o'clock. Tuvia was tired, but although he closed his eyes he didn't fall asleep.

The gate creaked. Soft footsteps came up the path. In front of the door the steps hesitated and stopped. He threw off the blanket and listened. There was a knock at the door. He looked at Hagar, but she was asleep. Again there was a faint knock. He didn't answer. He got out of bed, and walked barefoot to the kitchen door. He switched on the light and opened the door. In the darkness on the veranda he made out Sarah's short hair.

"Hello," he said.

"Oh, I'm sorry," she said. "I see that you're already in your pajamas. But I'm worried. Yiftach isn't back yet."

"He hasn't come home?"

"No. Hagar went for a walk with him this afternoon – perhaps he told her where he was going. I'm really worried."

"Hagar isn't feeling well. Do you think we should wake her?" He invited her in.

"I don't know. Perhaps, if it isn't too much trouble. I

don't know what to think. I haven't seen him since this morning. He came back with Bulkin. He went with her. And he isn't back yet. I don't know where to look for him. If it isn't too much trouble."

"Sit down," he said, "and don't worry. It's the first day of the vacation, perhaps the children are out playing now."

"I was at that lot where they play. There's nobody there. I went round to Tzemach's parents too. Tzemach was at home. And if that hooligan is at home, then none of the other children are still outside."

"All right," he said. "I'll go and wake her up."

Hagar appeared in her robe, sleepy.

"Excuse me for waking you," said Sarah.

"Never mind, it doesn't matter," Hagar yawned.

"But perhaps you know where Yiftach went after you went for a walk with him?"

Hagar sat down at the table. Tuvia stood next to the door.

"I'm so worried," said Sarah again. "He's never come home so late."

"I don't know where he went," said Hagar, "but don't worry. He's a big boy. He'll come home. He isn't with the other children?"

"No."

"So where can he be?"

"That's what I came to ask you!" cried Sarah.

"But I haven't seen him all day," said Hagar.

"You told me that you went for a walk with him, no? His canteen isn't on the table either."

"But I didn't go with him," said Hagar.

Sarah turned to the door and leaned against it. "I'm sorry I woke you up. But I thought, I thought that you saw him. You told me that you went for a walk with him. Didn't you see where he went after you left him?"

"Ah," sighed Hagar, "I really don't know." She went up to Sarah who was standing at the door, and took hold of her hand. "Don't worry, he'll come home," she said. The door was open and the mosquitoes flew in and hit her in the eyes. "Oof!" she cried, "Tuvia, why don't you shut the door?" There were tears in her eyes.

17

Tuvia didn't hear her shout. He left the house, after motioning Sarah to step aside from the door.

Outside in the yard he finished buttoning his shirt. He went out of the big gate, crossed the road, and knocked on the Strausses' door.

"Sarah?" he heard Simcha's hoarse voice.

"No, it's Erlich," he said.

"What's wrong?" Simcha asked as Tuvia came inside, his eyes red and his hair tousled.

"Nothing," said Tuvia. "I just woke up. Look," he continued, "perhaps you should come with me to Yoel's and we'll borrow his jeep. It's worrying. It's already half past ten, and Yiftach still hasn't come home."

"Ah, she's infected you with her panic too," said Simcha. "He'll come home. He's come home late before. It's the summer holidays. But she doesn't want to listen to me."

"Look," said Tuvia. "It's really late. I don't know, but she said that she went round to Tzemach's too. Even he's at home already."

Simcha stood next to the table. His brown leather bag full of greasy, empty lunch bags and a few tools was lying on the chair. He was unshaven, and above his full face his forehead was low and rough. He hadn't taken off his work clothes yet, and his socks hung sloppily over his shoes.

He mumbled something, picked up his bag and sat down on the chair. "I'm tired." He propped his elbow on the table and rested his head on his hand.

"So you don't think we should go and get the jeep?" asked Tuvia.

"Maybe we'd better," said Simcha. He stood up, went over to the window and looked outside. Then he went to the bathroom and came back in a clean shirt.

They went out into the road and at the gate they met Sarah. "Isn't he back yet?" she asked.

"No," said Simcha. "We're going to Yoel's, to take the jeep. We'll go and look for him."

"I'll come with you."

"There's no need," said Simcha. "You stay home, so that if he comes back there'll be somebody to give him what for."

They went on walking, but Sarah came with them.

"Go home," said Simcha, "there's no point in the three of us going, and someone has to stay home."

She went back and they walked on.

Yoel lived not far from the garage, at the other end of the village. It was a small house at the end of a group of crowded apartment buildings. In the dark it was hard to make it out.

"I've never walked to Yoel's before," said Tuvia. "It's as if I don't know the way."

"I think the lights are off," said Simcha.

"Too bad," said Tuvia, "we'll have to wake them up."

"Haven't you got the key to the jeep?"

"No, I don't need a key to start it, but I don't want to give them a fright."

"Who is it?" they heard a low voice. Yoel came out in his pajamas. He opened the door and put his finger to his lips as a sign to them not to make any noise. Tuvia and Simcha stood on the garden path.

"We need the jeep," said Tuvia.

"Is there anything wrong?" asked Yoel.

"No, nothing," said Simcha in his hoarse voice, "but Yiftach hasn't come home yet, and Sarah's worried."

"All right," said Yoel, "I'll come with you."

"There's no need," said Simcha.

As they talked a heavy shadow fell over them. It was Carmela, who had also woken up.

"Hasn't he come home yet?" she asked.

Carmela and Yoel went back inside. Simcha and Tuvia

got into the jeep, which was standing in the street next to the fence. Tuvia started it. The light went off in Yoel and Carmela's house.

"Where should we go, do you think?" asked Simcha.

"Don't you know where he liked to hang out?"

"Hard to know. Once he came home late. Last week, I think it was, but then he was at your place."

"At our place?"

"Yes, with Hagar."

Tuvia drove the jeep to the school building, which loomed up like a dark fort against the background of the light sky. The hedge that surrounded it was still, only the little leaves rippling when the lights of the jeep shone on them. The building was dark, but in the schoolyard, beneath the pine trees, there were shadows of children standing around a bonfire.

"He's such a bastard," said Simcha. "Sarah came home today worn out from the doctor, and that little one didn't even think of telling anybody where he was going, and when he meant to come home. I'll show him. Wait for me here," he said to Tuvia when the jeep stopped. "I'll be back in a minute."

"Don't make a scene in front of the children," said Tuvia.

"Don't worry," said Simcha.

He took out a cigarette and before going into the schoolyard he lit it.

In spite of the light breeze blowing into the jeep Tuvia felt tired, and leaned his head on the steering wheel.

When he woke up, he saw the tip of Simcha's cigarette burning in front of him. Before Simcha got into the jeep he threw the cigarette down, and ground it under his shoe.

"Did you leave him there?" asked Tuvia.

Simcha took the pack out of his pocket and lit himself another cigarette. "No," he said, "he wasn't there."

Simcha offered Tuvia a cigarette. But Tuvia shook his head, and Simcha said: "I forgot you don't smoke."

They drove along dirt roads and circled the village.

"They haven't seen him all day," said Simcha. "That is, they haven't spoken to him. They said he went to Bulkin, or to the Arab village. To Hagar."

"To Hagar?"

"Yes. They said she always walks there. And he goes with her."

"But Hagar told me that today she didn't go for a walk with him."

"Sarah said she did."

They drove past the plowed field with the dry furrows, climbed the hill, and drove along the fence of the cemetery.

"We're going to look for Yiftach," said Simcha, "but I can't stop thinking about Sarah."

The road was full of sand and Tuvia changed gears.

The abandoned *moshav* was in darkness, only the white walls shining. A lamp in the old watchman's house cast a pale light on the sagging fence. The dog barked. They parked the jeep next to the gate and went into the yard. The rope tied around the dog's neck was attached to a high laundry line and he ran up and down it, barking threateningly.

"Quiet, dog," an old man's voice roared. The watchman opened the window, stuck out his head and asked: "What do you want of my life in the middle of the night?"

"Have you seen Yiftach today?" asked Simcha.

"Yes, but a long time ago."

"Where?"

"What's up?"

"He hasn't come home yet."

"Ahh . . . " groaned the old man, "a fine kettle of fish. . . ." He vanished and they heard him call, "Just a minute, I'll be out in a minute."

He came out holding a flashlight and wearing a hat and a black scarf wrapped around his neck. He locked the door behind him, threw a piece of meat to the dog, and turned toward them.

"Women, women. . . ." he muttered and pointed at Tuvia. "I saw her today. I always see her wandering around. Sometimes with Yiftach. Sometimes by herself. Today with that soldier who lost his canteen. They went to the ruin next to the palms. Yiftach followed them. I don't know if they met. In the end she came back by herself. And him, Yiftach, I didn't see at all."

"Hagar?" said Tuvia. His face was tight and his lips hardly moved.

"Yes, your wife, your wife," said the old man. He

turned to the laundry line and untied the dog who finished gobbling down the meat. Then he scraped the ground with his paws, sniffed, hung his head and slunk after his master.

"Come along," said Simcha, "we'll go in the jeep."

"Where will we go in the jeep?" complained the watchman. "When you're looking for someone you have to go on foot. Leave the jeep here, and come along."

"Maybe he's already gone home," said Tuvia impatiently. "Where are we going anyway?"

"Look here," said the old watchman, "either you woke me up because you needed my help, or else you woke me up for nothing." He pulled the rope he was holding in his hand. "Quiet," he scolded the dog who had begun to growl.

A smell of dry mold came from the abandoned houses. They walked toward the palm trees, whose crowns in the dark looked like domed sepulchres fallen out of the sky. The old man walked ahead, dragging his feet, and also the dog, who kept stopping to sniff at the stones on the road.

"Do you know where we're going? " Simcha asked Tuvia.

"No."

"Maybe you're right, and Yiftach's already at home."

"I don't know what we're doing with this old man either."

"He saw Yiftach."

"Yes, and he saw Hagar too."

They walked slowly and fell behind the old man. The flashlight in his hand flickered and shed fitful beams of light onto the road and the deserted yards.

"We aren't doing this for fun," said the old man. "Get a move on. First you wake me up and now you're dawdling as if you've forgotten what you woke me up for. Oh, you youngsters. . . ."

The sky lightened and the trunks of the palms lining the road marched with them on their way like a guard of honor.

"Look," said the old man to Tuvia, "they must have gone to the Arab house with the pool. Maybe we'll find something there that will give us a clue where to look for him. He really hasn't come home all this time?"

"Not up till an hour ago, at any rate," said Tuvia.

"Yes. It's worrying. He could do something stupid. It's difficult to tell where the border runs. And especially for a little simpleton like Yiftach. Is that the way to leave a child? Oh, you're driving me crazy. First the soldiers come to the village and steal my pail and rope I left there to draw water from the well when I put the goat out to pasture. And she takes the child for walks out here, next to the railway line and the border. What kind of people are you? Where are your brains?"

"You said she didn't go with him," Tuvia interrupted. "You saw her alone with the soldier."

"All right, all right. Yes. But I wouldn't have said it if I'd seen you. I didn't see that it was you with Simcha at first."

"But she went with the soldier, right?" Tuvia almost shouted, and Simcha walking next to him turned his head back to the white houses which looked gray in the dark.

"Yes," said the old man. "And that doesn't add to your honor in my eyes."

"We'll discuss honor later," said Tuvia. "Where are you taking us now?"

"Look at them," said the old man. "First they wake me up and then they still ask questions."

They passed the yellow frontier sign, and the old watchman's flashlight shone on the solitary house with the dark, green plants creeping over its walls. Jackals howled in the orange grove and fireflies glittered between the leaves. The old man released the dog, who ran around the house with the short rope trailing behind him. When the dog returned to the front of the ruin he whimpered faintly and his whimper sounded like a distant echo of the jackals' wails. The flashlight picked out the doorway and penetrated the interior.

In the darkness the dirt on the colored tiles was invisible, and the ray of light wandering over them only occasionally revealed a dry branch, a rag, a clod of earth. The beam slid over the walls and stopped in the corner of the room, where it hit a burned brick lying next to the wall, and a heap of ragged sacks. Between the sacks and the brick lay a white bag embroidered in yellow thread.

The flashlight moved away from the embroidered bag and Tuvia said: "Shine the flashlight on that bag again."

And when the light poured over the bag again he went up to it and picked it up and said: "Yes, she was here." He opened the bag and put his hand into it. His fingers felt the wool, the needles, the sweater.

"Is it yours?" asked the old man.

"No, it's Hagar's," said Tuvia.

The old man went up to the ragged sacks and rummaged among them. "Maybe Yiftach left something here too," he said.

"Maybe," said Simcha, "but it doesn't look to me as if he was here at all."

The old man turned to Tuvia who was standing a little apart from Simcha, and whispered something in his ear. Afterward they both walked toward the doorway of the ruin.

"I have to tell Tuvia something." The old man went back to Simcha, and gave him the dog. "Look after him, we'll be back in a minute." Taken aback, Simcha moved closer to the wall, holding the rope in his hand.

With the flashlight shining in front of them they stepped onto a path leading between the trees. The old man took a packet of tobacco out of his pocket. The light veered off the path and skipped over the leaves.

"Do you smoke?" he asked Tuvia.

"No," said Tuvia. The old man stopped, rolled himself a cigarette, and stuck it together with his tongue. Then he lit the cigarette and said: "It's a pity you don't smoke."

They continued walking and he added hesitantly: "It's not because of that bag you found that I brought you here by yourself. What goes on between you and Hagar doesn't interest me, even though. . . ."

"Look here." Tuvia put his hand on the old man's shoulder and stopped him. "Shut up about Hagar. I think your eyes are too big."

"My eyes are an old man's eyes, but your eyes, young man, are too small." The cigarette was stuck in the corner of his mouth. "Never mind that," he added immediately. "I think the business with Yiftach is serious. I told him myself that Hagar had come here. I met him in the Arab village. He was playing with his new canteen. I met Hagar too. But she came back alone."

"And where was the soldier?"

"I didn't see him."

The old man stepped off the path, and Tuvia followed him into a tangle of branches and leaves which brushed against his clothes and tugged at his hair. The light ran over the ground and revealed dry leaves.

"It's happened before," said the old man when they reached a little clearing among the trees. He switched the flashlight off.

"What's happened before?"

"That a child disappeared. It was long ago. You know there's an army camp not far from here. It used to be a British camp. I worked there as a builder. Your father worked there too, when he was a cart-driver. He transported rocks from the quarry to the camp. No question about it, he did good business. Well, never mind that. There were a few British officers living here. The son of one of them went for a walk and got lost."

The old man lit the flashlight and shone it onto the opening of a water hole dug in the middle of the clearing. Weeds covered the edges of the pit. "Here, in this well, which still worked then, they found him. The child. That's why I brought you here." They approached the edge of the pit. The flashlight shone on a rusty ladder.

"Take the flashlight. And go down the ladder. Don't be afraid. There's no water in the well. They blocked it up with stones. But we should check it out. I'm sure that if we go back now, Yiftach won't be at home. I know those scamps. Roaming all over the place."

Tuvia was silent. A sharp cold flooded his face. He moved closer to the edge of the pit and looked inside. Long iron rods stuck out of the soil. "It's not deep," he heard the old man's voice. "Go on down." He gripped the ladder and began descending rung after rung. The ladder vanished into the stones blocking up the well. He stopped. With one hand he clung to the ladder, and with the other he shone the flashlight on the walls. He felt a heavy pressure on his ears. It was hot. His face was sweating. The dust of all kinds of junk clouded his eyes: tins, cement blocks, broken crates. There was a smell of rotten oranges. An iron pole leaned against the wall of the well, next to the ladder. He pulled the pole toward him and poked about in the junk with it. He pushed sacks out of the way, moved planks. The pit filled with dust. He didn't find anything. He shoved the flashlight into his belt and climbed up the ladder. He was choking on the dust and felt that his undershirt was soaked with sweat.

A gust of cold lashed his damp face as he poked his head out of the pit. The old man held out his hand to help him up. "Nothing," said Tuvia. "There's nothing down there."

He returned the flashlight to the old man, who gave him Hagar's bag. "Good," said the old man. "Let's go back and drive to Simcha's place. Please God the boy's already home. I'm afraid, afraid." They walked back along the path.

"Don't say anything to Simcha yet," Tuvia warned the old man.

"Don't worry."

The main road was empty. The streetlights were out. Their street was deserted too, but when they approached the gate of Tuvia's house a woman ran out to them. It was Sarah. The dog barked.

Tuvia parked the jeep at the side of the road, and Sarah ran straight to Simcha. The old man looked at Tuvia, who was leaning against the warm engine hood.

"Well?" she asked.

"Hasn't he come home yet?" asked Tuvia.

"No," said Sarah. She came up to him and said quietly: "You should teach your wife to tell the truth. She's a liar."

"Quiet," said Simcha.

"What quiet? This afternoon she said that she went for a walk with him. This evening, when he didn't come back, she said she didn't. I'm sure she's hiding something. It doesn't make sense that he hasn't come home yet. And don't tell me to keep quiet, I want to know where he is. And you too," she turned to Tuvia, "if you want to stick up for her, then go to her. We don't need you here."

"I think that Yiftach ate at our house more than once," said Tuvia, "and Hagar was always very good to him. I don't know what you want of her."

Tuvia felt the old man's hand tighten around his arm.

Silence descended on the street.

Only the dog ran around the old man, sniffing the ground, and then climbed up his legs, scratching his trousers. In Tuvia's house, in the bathroom, the light went out. The distant sound of a car engine reached them.

Sarah was silent. She went into their yard and walked slowly to the front door. Simcha looked at the motionless jeep and followed his wife.

"There's nothing to do now," the old man said to his receding back, "but if he doesn't come home, go to the police."

"Thank you," said Simcha without turning his head.

"Look after her," said the old man and pointed to Sarah.

Tuvia got into the jeep. "Come on, get in," he said to the old man. "I'll take you home."

"No need," said the old man. "I'll walk."

The shadows of the old man and the dog disappeared up the street. Tuvia parked the jeep in the yard, shut the gate and went inside.

18

In front of the door he paused for a moment. His undershirt was still wet with sweat. In his hand he held Hagar's knitting bag. The veranda light was on. Mosquitoes swarmed around the naked bulb above him. A bad smell came from his work shoes standing on the marble ledge. He went into the kitchen. There were two empty coffee cups on the table.

Hagar was lying in bed, awake. She looked at him when he came into the room, but she didn't say hello.

"I've brought you something," he said.

"Did Yiftach come back?"

Tuvia threw the bag onto the bed.

"You were there today, in that Arab house, weren't you?"

There was a gray thread from one of the sacks in the ruined house sticking to the knitting bag. Hagar was covered with the thin, white summer coverlet, and only her head was sticking out.

"Yes. But I only saw him. It's not true that I went for a walk with him."

"With whom?"

"Has Yiftach come back?"

"I think I asked you a question."

Hagar took the unfinished sweater out of the knitting bag. Tuvia went on standing by the door.

"No," he said, "he hasn't come back."

She rolled the ball of wool over the bed and played

with the knitting needles. The sweater lay on the pillow, next to her head. "Aren't you tired?" she asked.

He came up and sat down on the bed.

"You shouldn't have lied to her," he said.

"I looked for him all day. Ask Bulkin. I was confused. I only saw him for a minute. What a day. . . ."

"Did you go to the school?"

"No, I'll go tomorrow."

"And what did you do today?"

"Why don't we go to sleep," she said.

He looked at his watch. It was a quarter to one. "And I have to go to work in the morning," he said and took off his shoes.

"You've got grass on your shirt." She bent over him and brushed off the grass.

"Sarah's cross with me too," he said.

"She's cross with the whole world."

"Maybe she's right."

"But someone should be on my side too in all this argument."

"There's no argument," said Tuvia. "She left Yiftach with you. And he hasn't come home yet."

"She didn't leave him with me. He went to Acre with Bulkin this morning."

"And who's the soldier you were with in the *moshav?*"

"Do you really want to know?"

Tuvia didn't answer. His pajamas were lying on the bed and he took off his shirt and put it on the chair. When he was dressed in his pajamas he went to the window and looked out. There was a light on in Simcha and Sarah's house. His throat was dry, and Hagar looked at him and asked: "Would you like me to make you something to drink?" She got up and went to the kitchen.

His hair felt dry, even though he had washed his face. He was very tired. He sat on a chair in the kitchen, leaning against the wall, and his hand holding the glass of tea trembled. He drank, set the glass down on the table and put his hands on his knees.

"Do you think there's any danger?" Hagar stirred the sugar into her tea. The teaspoon hit the glass and made a tinkling sound.

"I haven't got the strength to get up," he said and with the help of his hands leaning on the table he rose to his feet and walked to the bedroom. He got into bed, and in spite of the light on in the room he closed his eyes and tried to fall asleep. There was a knock at the door again.

Hagar opened the door. It was Simcha.

"Sorry," he said. "This is the third time we've woken you up tonight. But. . . .."

"Never mind," said Hagar.

"Is Tuvia asleep already?"

"No," Tuvia called from the bedroom. "What's up?"

Simcha came in. He was still in his work clothes, and his unshaven face was covered with stubble.

"I'm sorry about disturbing you," he said. His red eyes wandered over the room. "I think we should inform the police. Sarah's crying all the time."

Sarah was waiting for them in the street, and Simcha gave her the seat next to Tuvia.

In Kasos's cafe the light was still on.

"Go and ask him," Sarah said to Simcha.

"What for," said Simcha. "Yiftach's not there."

"Of course he's not there, but maybe Kasos knows something."

"There's no need to drive the whole world crazy."

Tuvia stopped the jeep. "Go on," he said to Simcha. "Words don't cost money."

Simcha hesitated and then got slowly out of the jeep. The light pouring out of the cafe fell onto the paving stones of the sidewalk and onto the round pillar with the notices and posters pasted onto it. Kasos had already turned the chairs up onto the tables, and he was sweeping the floor. When he saw Simcha coming he went up to the door and leaned on the broom to wait for him. They exchanged a few words, and Simcha returned to the jeep. Tuvia and Sarah didn't ask any questions. Tuvia started the jeep. There seemed to be nothing on the sides of the road as they drove. No houses, no trees, just darkness and desolation.

The police station was dark too, with only two lights on next to the fence. A patrol car pulled onto the road. The eucalyptus trees were tangled and silent. They couldn't see the bars of the detention cells on the ground floor. The telephone operator was sitting next to the switchboard, his arms crossed on the long, high counter. His head was resting on his arms, and his eyes were closed.

All three of them entered the waiting room, but it was Sarah who spoke. She went up to the operator, touched his arm, and roused him.

"What do you want?" He woke up. He put on his hat and eyeglasses, which were lying to one side.

"My little boy hasn't come home all day," said Sarah. Her dress was creased.

"So what do you want me to do, bring him home?" He picked up a pencil. The telephone rang.

"It's so late. I haven't seen him all day."

"Just a minute," said the policeman, and picked up the telephone receiver.

"So what do you want? Tonight nobody can look for him. We have to wait till tomorrow."

"But you can do something, can't you?" said Tuvia.

"Not tonight. It's dark."

"And when will you come tomorrow?"

"In the morning."

"So what are you police for?" asked Sarah.

"Don't shout please, lady."

He took a form and held the pencil poised over it.

"Have you looked in all the places he usually frequents?"

"Yes," said Tuvia.

"How old is he?"

"Ten," said Sarah.

"Height?"

"A meter thirty-eight."

"Fat? Thin?"

"Thin."

"What color eyes?"

"Green."

"Hair?"

"Brown."

"Clothes?"

"A blue knit shirt. Short khaki pants. Sandals."

"Distinguishing characteristics?"

"A canteen."

"On his body, I mean. Like a scar, or a birthmark."

"No. But he apparently had a canteen on him."

"Languages?"

"What languages! He's ten years old!"

The policeman wrote down the details.

The old watchman walked slowly down the dirt track. The dog dragged behind him, tired. The air was clear, and the darkness gave it a chill. On the corner he stopped and rolled himself a cigarette. In the distance he saw the figure of a man. When it came nearer, he saw by the can of glue hanging from its hand that it was Noah Bulkin. The old man stood and smoked. The dog wagged his tail and ran into the avenue.

Bulkin stopped next to one of the trees and pasted a yellow poster onto its trunk. When he saw the old watchman, he crossed the road and went up to him.

"Is it nice to stick up posters in the middle of the night, like a thief?" the old man scolded him.

"And when the police beat up workers in the port in broad daylight, is that nice?" retorted Bulkin.

The dog came back and began sniffing the glue.

"And what are you doing here now?" asked Bulkin.

"Going for a walk. Getting a breath of air."

"Precisely here?"

"Tell Hilmi that I'm out of tobacco." The old man didn't answer the question. "Tell him to bring a few bags."

"All right. But in the meantime why don't you roll me one too?"

The old man rolled Bulkin a cigarette, and they walked on together.

Before they parted, Bulkin asked again: "Has something happened?"

The old man shook his head. "I don't know yet. Why waste words for nothing?"

19

In the morning the neighbors came out of their yards and gathered outside Sarah's house. The police car drove up with its siren wailing. It parked in the middle of the crowd. Two policemen got out and pushed their way to the gate.

"Let them through! Let them through!"

Hagar stood at the window and through the net of people standing in the street she saw Sarah. One of the policemen held her by the arm and escorted her though the crowd. The other one, who was short and fat, cleared the way with his baton.

Simcha came out too. He walked slowly to the gate, shook hands with Tabak, who shook his head and mumbled something, and joined Sarah as she talked to the policeman. The sun detached itself from the blue mountains in the east. The grayness of the morning disappeared, but the light above Sarah and Simcha Strauss's front door went on shining.

Sarah pointed at Hagar's house. The policeman turned to look in the direction of her pointing finger, and Hagar moved away from the window. When she looked out through the screen again she saw the policeman leaving Sarah and Simcha and turning toward her house. The crowd followed him, and a muffled wave of whispers spread through the street. A second police car drove up and stopped outside the house. A few policemen got out, two of them holding dogs on leashes.

Tuvia had hardly slept all night. In the morning he had returned the jeep to Yoel and announced that he wouldn't be coming to work. He had promised Simcha to help in the search.

Hagar was still in her nightgown, and the house hadn't been tidied up. When she saw the policeman approaching the house, she went to the bathroom and washed her face, changed her clothes and tied her hair up in white ribbons. She closed the bedroom door and cleared away the newspaper from the table in the hall. The shutters were open, but the stuffiness which had accumulated in the rooms during the night had not yet dispersed. Without waiting for the policeman to knock on the door, she went out onto the veranda to meet him.

"Perhaps we should go inside," he suggested.

They sat down at the table. Hagar wanted to offer him some refreshments, but before she could utter a word she heard the policeman say: "You'd better tell me everything, without leaving any details out. A child's life is at stake here."

Hagar was speechless. She squeezed her hands between her legs. The ribbons in her hair gave her face a childishly embarrassed look.

The policeman's hair was smooth and combed back. There was a black mustache, sprinkled with gray, above his thick lips. His cap rested on his knees.

"You went for a walk with him yesterday. When you left him, where did he go? What did you talk about? Did he mention anywhere that he wanted to go?"

"I didn't go for a walk with him," she said.

"You walked right next to the border. They say you even passed the yellow sign. The warning sign. Perhaps he crossed the border. We have to know every detail."

"But I told you, I don't know anything. I didn't go for a walk with him. I never managed to meet up with him."

"Mrs. Strauss says that she left the child with you."

"I don't know what she wants of me. I love Yiftach too. You'd better begin looking for him. Believe me, I didn't see him. That is, I didn't go for a walk with him yesterday."

"But you did see him?"

"Look. . . . What do you want of me?"

"Just answer my questions."

"My husband and Sarah's husband didn't sleep the

whole night. They were out searching for Yiftach. I think that's what you were called in for too. To search for Yiftach, not to waste time on me."

"You said you saw him. Where?"

"Near the *moshav*."

"What were you doing there?"

"What's it got to do with you?"

"Just answer the question. Impertinence won't help you. What were you doing there?"

"Going for a walk."

"Who with?"

Hagar undid one of the ribbons in her hair and wrapped it around her hand. A cool breeze blew through the open windows, but her face was hot and flushed.

"Who with?" the policeman repeated his question.

She didn't answer.

"Every minute is precious to us, and you're deliberately evading my questions." The policeman stood up and went over to the window.

"I was alone."

"But you were seen with someone else."

"Not with Yiftach."

"So you didn't go for a walk with him?"

"With whom?"

"You should know."

"I went for a walk alone. I told you. I saw Yiftach suddenly, before I came back. He was in the orange grove beside the *moshav*."

"Are you sure?"

There were rapid footsteps on the veranda. They were silent as the door opened. "You're still here?" It was Tuvia. He looked at the policeman who was still standing next to the window. "It's already eight o'clock. I thought you'd already started doing something."

The policeman went out. Before closing the door he said: "I haven't finished yet. But that's enough for now."

"What did he want of you?" asked Tuvia.

"Exactly the same as what you want."

She opened the door of the bedroom and threw herself onto the bed. "I've got no strength left," she said.

"Come on," Tuvia bent over her, "you come too."

"I'm tired," she said.

"I want Sarah to see that you've got nothing against her, that it wasn't your fault. Come on."

"I've got no strength left," she said again. "How can I help? I'm going to sleep. Afterward I'll go and do the shopping. You'll come home for lunch. Will you come?"

Tuvia left. Hagar stayed in bed. It was suffocating in the bedroom again. The shutters were closed. She stood up. Her legs trembled. The echo of the neighbors' commotion rose from the street. She opened the shutters. The window screen was dusty. The siren of the patrol car receded in the distance. The voices of the people scattered. Clear, exhausting air flowed into the room. She got back into bed. The white ribbon tickled her throat and she closed her eyes. Fully dressed she tossed and turned under the covers. The street was quiet. The milkman passed with his donkey. She had forgotten to put the bottles out. She heard his steps on the path. He put the milk on the veranda balustrade and knocked on the door. She did nothing. He waited a few seconds and left. She heard the gate creak, the whip cracking on the donkey's back. Her eyes were still closed, and the milkman's gray beard filled them. She couldn't fall asleep. But neither could she get up and bring in the milk bottles.

The smell of the soldier's shirt filled her nostrils. On the shelf of the bedside table she saw the knitting bag. At first she turned her eyes away from it, but then she jumped out of bed. Again he hadn't said anything to her. She drank a cup of coffee, brought in the milk, and smoothed the creases in her clothes.

She went to the school. She walked with her eyes downcast. From time to time she heard the siren of a patrol car. The street was quiet. Women came out of the shops with heavy baskets. Among the ruins of the Arab village she saw the people and the policemen, appearing and disappearing behind the tumbledown walls of the houses, the stone walls. Next to the olive trees stood two policemen, leaning over the hood of a jeep, studying maps.

The schoolyard was full of children. The teachers were organizing the children in rows, while the principal circled among them with a tin megaphone in his hands. From time to time muffled cries came from the megaphone: "Fifth grade! Form up next to the ladder." When she walked past the gate it seemed to her that they were all staring at her, and she stopped behind an old ficus tree and waited. She didn't go into the schoolyard, and in the end she went home. On the main road she saw Hilmi driving a cart harnessed to Bulkin's new mule. It trotted down the road, and she turned toward Tabak's grocery store.

The sound of soldiers' singing rose in her ears. An open truck full of soldiers drove past the square, as if it were chasing Hilmi's cart. She remembered how he asked her: "Will you be here tomorrow too?" She couldn't remember what she had said. She went into the grocery store, where she was the only customer. Simcha Strauss's shop, in the main street, was shut. There was a white cardboard notice hanging on the door.

"Did you want something?" Tabak's wife wiped her broad hands on her apron. She was fat, the skin of her face drawn into a close net of fine wrinkles. Her little eyes lashed Hagar. She stood next to the bread cupboard and set the little scales on the counter.

Hagar went up to the counter. The smell of smoked fish rose in her nostrils. She didn't have her basket with her.

"Didn't you join them?" Tabak's wife asked.

When her purchases piled up on the counter Hagar asked for a bag. "That'll cost you two grosch," said Mrs. Tabak. She didn't help Hagar to pack the things into the bag. She put her change down on the counter, and retired to the back room without saying good-bye.

Hagar walked slowly up the street, holding the heavy paper bag with both hands, pressed against her chest.

The school children, formed up in rows, were marching

in the direction of the Arab village. Sarah and Simcha Strauss's yard was empty. The dry grass bowed over the ground. The laundry line was bare and limp.

She straightened up the house, swept the rooms, washed the kitchen floor. She laundered Tuvia's work clothes, and then she left the house and walked to the Arab village. Tuvia had been put in charge of a group of civilians. She joined him. Mr. Tabak greeted her politely. In the distance, near the group of policemen, Bulkin and Hilmi were driving in the old Morris. Next to the olive trees stood a police car with a radio transmitter. Trackers followed dogs who kept their noses to the ground. She didn't see Sarah. Simcha was walking beside one of the policemen.

The policemen divided the territory into areas, and put groups of pupils and civilians in charge of searching them. They combed the ruined houses one by one and searched for hidden wells among the stones and bushes. They raised sheets of rusty old tin covering furnaces choked with sand. Everybody said: "He must have crossed the border."

Two UN vehicles, white with black lettering, drove down the road, entered the *moshav,* crossed the stretch of road marked as the frontier, and drove toward the first Arab village on the other side. In the afternoon police-men appeared on the other side of the border too. The peasants who had been bending over the plowed fields in the morning had disappeared.

Far from them all, next to the railway line, between the

eucalyptus trees surrounding the army camp, she saw the old *moshav* watchman walking behind his dog. The search advanced in a northerly direction. Late in the afternoon they were notified from the other side of the border that for the time being there was no news. Toward nightfall the searching stopped. The next morning they resumed. This went on for four days. From day to day the number of people participating in the search parties decreased. And on the last day it was only the policemen, Simcha, Tuvia, and the old watchman. Sarah was not yet wearing black stockings. She sat at home and waited.

On the other side of the border too the searching had stopped. "We'll notify you when the body's found," they were informed through the UN officers.

"I'm looking forward to your vacation," said Hagar to Tuvia when the search was over.

"Me too," he said. "But if you want to rest, why don't you go and spend some time at home."

In the afternoon Sarah would sit on the doorstep. She would look at the weeds wilting in the sun. One day she started going to Kasos's for supper. She always went in the same black dress decorated with white flowers, the dress in which she had returned from Dr. Volowitz to the house empty of both her sons. She didn't take the bus to the institution to visit her baby, and she didn't believe that Yiftach's fate was sealed. She didn't say "He'll be back" to anyone, but she didn't mourn for him either, and she would sometimes mention him in conversation.

Simcha worked less in the shop and came home early in the afternoon. They could sometimes be seen in the yard. Working. Pulling out the weeds, pruning the trees, painting the doors, cleaning out the shed.

Once in a while a policeman would come to their house, go over scraps of information and various ideas with them, express his sympathy and regrets, and go away again.

In her hopes Sarah was helped by Bulkin, who told Simcha, when he came to install electricity in the stable, that Hilmi always went home on foot, in order to go on searching all the time. He searched beside the army camp, in the orange groves, in the fields.

Many days had already passed since the day when Yiftach disappeared. The eucalyptus tree in the empty lot was swarming with children again, and the sun warmed the sand as if nothing had happened. Sarah and Simcha took their evening meal at Kasos's cafe. Hagar went to the principal of the school and offered herself as a teacher. The principal's tone was reserved. "Go ahead and study," he said. "If there's an opening I'll take you. Although, you must understand, in the light of what happened. . . . I don't know how the parents will react. But of course you should study. And do the examinations. Perhaps I can arrange something for you in some neighboring village." Suddenly his face took on a cheerful expression, and he stood up and looked into the mirror next to the window, and ran his slender pink fingers over his gray hair.

"Thank you," she said. The headmaster escorted her to the door. And with his hand on her waist he said: "If you run into any problems with your studies, come to me. I'm always here, and I'll be glad to help you."

At Tabak's too they seemed to have forgotten, and when she once again forgot her shopping basket, Mrs. Tabak gave her a brown paper bag without saying, "It'll cost you two grosch." And with her little eyes fixed on the floor she helped Hagar pack her purchases into the bag.

Hagar would sometimes go for a walk in the Arab village, alone. The soldiers had suddenly disappeared, and apart from the distant eucalypti touching the sky there was nothing to remember them by.

20

One day she got a letter from him. The pages were creased and the pencil blunt. But the writing was clear, the lines straight. There were dirty fingerprints on the envelope. She stood still on the path, not far from the mailbox. The letter surprised her. There was another letter too, but Hagar only opened his letter. Through the branches of the lilac the sun beat down on her. A strange voice pulsed in her heart. She didn't take in everything she read. The smell of his sweat rose again in her nostrils.

In her hands she felt his rough black boots. She didn't remember Yiftach's little fingers climbing up the window. She walked slowly along the path, folded the page and read.

There was no return address on the back of the envelope. She went into the house, and closed the shutters. In spite of the darkness in the room, she read the letter again. It was only then that she opened the other letter. It was from Tuvia's sister. She had given birth to another son. The letter included an invitation to the *brit*.

She had forgotten that she had made an appointment with the school principal at eleven o'clock. She had to fill in forms. The chances of her employment had increased. No substitute had yet been found for Esther Schmerling, the teacher who had died a few weeks before the end of the school year. She gathered up her books which were scattered over the table, and put them on the sewing machine. In the bathroom she inspected herself. The lines in her cheeks had grown deeper. She closed her mouth and pressed her lips together. She felt weak. The letter was in the pocket of her dress.

It was Friday. The previous day, before she fell asleep, Tuvia had asked her: "What do you want of life?"

"What makes you ask that now?"

"I have a bad feeling."

"Because of me?"

"Because of both of us," he said. His eyes were fixed on the white tablecloth. His hand trembled. Hagar knew that Tuvia and Yoel had expanded the garage, taken on new workers.

"I don't understand," she said.

"Don't you?"

"My head aches," she said. He sat on the other side of the table and she held out her hand to him.

It was evening, after their meal. They went straight to bed. In bed nothing happened. Tuvia kissed her and she lay still. But now, although she pushed her hand into her pocket and felt the dry pages of the letter, she would have been ready to respond to his caresses of last night. She saw the empty schoolyard. The janitor cleaning the corridors where no child's footsteps had trodden for many days, pushing the straw bristles over the gray tiles and the wet rag over the windowpanes dusty with the summer sand. In the kitchen, on the marble counter, in a bowl of water, were peeled potatoes. On the sewing machine were her books. She changed her dress, drank a glass of cold water, and went to the school. It was half past twelve, and she hoped that the principal was still there.

But at the gate she met the janitor, who was tall and stooped, his back humped.

"The principal's already left," he said.

"Did he leave a long time ago?"

"He waited for you until about a quarter of an hour ago." The janitor was holding a short-handled rake and raking up dry pine needles into a rubber basket.

"Why didn't you come on time?" He went on working as he spoke.

"Isn't he coming back in the afternoon?" asked Hagar.

"No," said the janitor. "He won't be coming back until school starts."

Instead of going back to the main road Hagar turned

into the plowed field between the schoolyard and the cemetery. The dry mounds didn't glitter in the sun – they were cracked, wilted. The gravedigger passed between the tombstones, watering the flowers, strengthening the supports of the creepers, collecting the dry leaves and scraps of paper strewn over the ground. Hagar walked slowly along the fence, and when she stepped onto the sunlit main road she was seized by a feeling of loneliness. The road was empty, and she felt as if she were exposed to view. She began to run. With short steps, her head lowered, she came on toward the houses of the Arab village.

When she reached the shade of the cypress avenue she stopped. Between the end of the cypresses and the old railway station the ground was yellow with the sun again, and there she saw him. He stood up and walked toward her.

"I thought you wouldn't come," he said.

Hagar panted for breath. She smiled. "Come, let's go to the cypress trees," she said.

The ground was padded with leaves and grass. They leaned against two rough trunks.

"I got your letter," she said without looking at him. "I didn't want to come. But I wanted to tell you something."

"What?"

"That I can't come any more."

The soldier twisted around and sat down facing her. He raised himself to his knees with one hand leaning against the tree trunk. The shadow falling on him was dappled.

Rough streaks of sunlight divided his body. "Why?" he asked. "I'm not what you think."

"It's not that," she said. "I have obligations."

"Are you married?"

"Didn't you know?"

"At first I thought you were. But after you said that the kid you were with wasn't yours, I understood that you weren't." He fixed his eyes on her and immediately looked away. Again he sat with his back leaning against the trunk of the tree. He took a pack of cigarettes out of his shirt pocket.

"Do you smoke?"

"No," she said, "but I'll have one."

The smoke spiraled in front of their faces in thick, dense clouds. There was no wind and it took a long time to disperse. The soldier sat next to her, hunched up, his hands on his knees. Hagar coughed.

"I can't smoke it." She put the cigarette out. "Do you want to keep what's left?"

"No," he said, "throw it away."

She threw the cigarette away. A narrow ribbon of thin smoke rose from it.

The soldier watched the smoke rising from the unfinished cigarette. Hagar put her hand on his shoulder. "Don't be angry with me," she said.

A car drove past on the road, and after the noise faded they heard the sound of a whip cracking on an animal's back. Iron cart wheels clattered over the asphalt.

"How old are you?" he asked.

She was silent.

"When I saw you with the kid," he said, "you seemed older to me. Now, without him, you look young."

Her hand between his stiffened. The smoke rising from the cigarette between his lips got into her eyes. She freed her hand and rose to her feet.

"Did something happen?"

"What do you mean?"

"Did something happen to you?"

"Yes. But it's got nothing to do with you."

Her eyes were damp, and when he took her hand again, she put her head on his shoulder and hugged him.

They walked along the avenue, in the shade of the trees falling on the field.

"That little boy," she said, "he disappeared."

"What do you mean, disappeared?"

They stepped onto the road.

"Go now," she said.

"Will you come tomorrow?"

"I don't know. I don't think so."

The soldier walked away. A car coming from the direction of the abandoned *moshav* emitted thick smoke from its exhaust and hid him from her. The sweat trickling down Hagar's face washed the mascara from her eyes and left two dark stripes on her cheeks.

The sun hit the dry grass, and at the edge of the orange grove, on the road leading to Noah Bulkin's house, she saw Hilmi. He was standing up in the new cart to which the mule was harnessed and cracking his whip on the beast's glossy brown back. The mule broke into a gallop and the whip traced swift circles over its head.

21

In spite of the long line of customers, Tabak left the shop on Friday afternoon and crossed the road to Kasos's cafe. "Don't leave me alone with this line!" his wife cried after him, but he had already disappeared.

Next to the sidewalk opposite the cafe he could already see Mizrachi's kerosene cart. Itzkowitz, the bill-poster with his thick canvas knapsack, his pail of glue, and his big brush had already gone inside. On Friday afternoon everyone was there. Even Hilmi came sometimes, but this time Tabak didn't see him. Kasos put the box of dominoes out on the table, but nobody played. They discussed the soccer match that was going to be played on Saturday. They took the teams apart and put them together again, read the sports paper, and compared the standings of the teams in the league.

When the arguments grew fiercer Tabak took the dominoes out of the box, scattered them over the table, and began playing against himself. Tabak was a religious man. But this didn't stop him from going to the soccer matches on Saturday. He bought the tickets from Itzkowitz, the bill-poster, on Friday afternoons. Now too he took out his wallet, and Itzkowitz gave him a ticket.

As he put the ticket in his pocket Sarah came into the cafe. Tabak collected the dominoes lying scattered over the table and built two towers equal in height with them. He took his hat which was hanging on the back of the chair, and put it on his head. An old violin tune creaked on the gramophone. Tabak removed his hat, put it on his knees, and the dominoes fell down onto the table. Kasos brought Sarah a cup of black coffee.

Sarah was wearing the same dress she always wore. The white flowers on the black dress seemed to have yellowed, wilted with dust. Her hair was no longer short. She had let it grow wild, and it fell in heavy waves round the nape of her neck.

Tabak stood up, his double chin trembled, and even the wrinkles on his face seemed to collide with each other. The sports newspaper in Itzkowitz's hand fell to the floor, and when he bent to pick it up Tabak trod on it, and it tore. Tabak went up to Sarah, held out his hand to her, and said: "How are you, Sarah?" Sarah was startled, and the coffee cup in her hand shook. Black drops trickled down its sides.

All eyes were turned to the street. The trunk of the pine tree opposite the counter was dry. But Sarah thought she could see a few shoots, small and green, sprouting from it. On the sidewalk outside, slowly, with her head bowed, Hagar walked past.

The record stopped playing, but went on turning round, creaking faintly. Tabak averted his face from the window. He saw Hagar turning toward his grocery store, and he sat down next to Sarah.

"Why don't you turn off that gramophone?" he said to Kasos. "Can't you hear that it's getting on everybody's nerves with its scraping?"

"Right away," said Kasos. He went up to the gramophone and turned the record over. The sobbing of the violin filled the cafe again.

Hagar disappeared into Tabak's grocery store, and the din in the cafe was renewed.

Kasos looked at Sarah's glass coffee cup. The sides were streaked with brown stripes. And when their eyes met, he saw a glint in her eyes that he had never seen there before.

22

When she heard Tuvia's jeep entering the yard, Hagar went back into the kitchen.

On Friday afternoon the sun had a special color. The streets gradually emptied of people, and the sand became lighter and cleaner. It seemed to her that even the dry grass stood a little straighter, imbued with a spark of life. That's how it always was. But now, when she heard Tuvia's heavy steps, and when she looked outside, she saw that the shutters in Sarah's house were closed, there was no washing on the line, and the grass underneath the windows was dry and wilted.

It was not until the evening, when they were eating, that she said to him: "I have to tell you something."

"Tell me," he said.

"Not now," she suddenly refused, "later."

Tuvia said nothing and she didn't say any more. After a few minutes he asked:

"When later?"

"We got a letter from your sister," she said.

"Has she had the baby?"

"Yes."

"What?"

"A boy."

Tuvia stood up, went to the window, came back, and said: "Why don't we go and see them tomorrow?"

"Tomorrow already?"

"Why not? Did you buy them something this afternoon?"

"No," she said, "I think we should wait for the *brit*."

"Have you got something against her?"

"No."

"So why shouldn't we go tomorrow?"

"I don't know."

After the meal they went out for a walk. They walked along the deserted main road in the direction of the police station. They passed the garage, and Tuvia told her that everything was going well. They had sold another used truck. Soon they would start painting car windows with a special color against the sun. "Altogether, we have plenty of plans," he said, "but it's not always clear to me who all this work is for."

"What do you mean who it's for?"

"What will I do with it all?"

"I don't understand you," she said, "what do people work for?"

"My father, for example, had something to work for."

"What?"

"Me, all of us."

Her lips closed. A solitary car illuminated them in its headlights, and when the noise of its engine had died away, they heard the sound of their own footsteps on the asphalt. They left the main road and walked along the dirt track winding between the orange grove and the new housing projects. A wind blew, and white summer clouds covered the sky. A little girl's head popped out of one of the lighted windows opposite them.

"You may still get what you want," she said. A sharp, brief laugh cut into her words. She stopped and pushed the hair out of her eyes. The lights in the house opposite them went out, and the head of the little girl disappeared.

"Is that what you wanted to tell me?"

"Not exactly. But it's connected."

Tuvia grabbed her arm and pulled her to him. "Look at me," he said.

They were back on the main road again. Children riding bicycles passed them and stopped next to the notice board. The wind died down, and only the clouds went on blanketing the sky and covering the stars. A stifling heat began coming down. Hagar was sweating. "I don't feel well," she said.

"What's the matter?"

"I don't know. I feel weak in my legs, my whole body."

"So you won't come with me tomorrow?"

"That's it then? You've decided?"

"Come home and rest now, and tomorrow we'll drive up to Jerusalem. A change of air will do us good."

"Go on your own," she said.

"Why?"

"Go on your own. I don't feel well. Besides, I want to stay at home on my own for a bit."

"And every day, you're not on your own?"

"Tomorrow it will be something different."

"Something different . . . " he repeated.

"When you come back, I'll have something to tell you."

The lights in the square were on, casting bright spots on the street. The shops were closed and the sidewalk under the avenue of ficus trees was deserted. Only in Kasos's cafe was the light on, and his stooped silhouette was visible through the dusty window. The hoarse strains of a violin came from the gramophone, accompanied by someone singing in a low voice. It was Bulkin, who was sitting next to a glass of beer and waiting for his supper.

Between the trees they saw Sarah and Simcha Strauss. Simcha was wearing a white shirt, but Sarah had not changed her dress. Simcha had his arm around her, but her arms were hanging limply by her sides. They were going to Kasos's, to eat. Hagar and Tuvia passed them in silence.

"Why don't you tell me now?" asked Tuvia before they went to sleep.

"Turn off the light," she said.

23

Hagar sweated all night.

At midnight, Tuvia made her tea. She had a fever. The air in the room was damp and muggy. They fell asleep again. Tuvia woke up early. Hagar's forehead was dry and cool. Beside the lines on her cheeks were streaks of dried sweat. Her body was covered with the sheet and only her face peeped out.

Outside there was a Sabbath morning silence. Tuvia sat on the edge of the bed, with his bare feet touching the floor. He looked at her.

"I feel fine," she said. "Go, and come back quickly."

"Are you sure you feel all right?"

"I'm not sweating any more."

"We'll go together, for the *brit*," he said.

Her head didn't move. Her eyes were fixed on the white ceiling. Little by little, between the slats of the shutters, daylight crept into the room and revealed her features, the contours of her body covered by the sheet, which was stained with yellow spots of sweat.

"Go," she said again. She took her eyes from the ceiling and looked at him.

He pushed his feet into his slippers, moved up to her, and put his hand on her forehead. "Another time," he said. "I'll stay with you today."

She kissed his hand. "There's no need," she whispered. "Truly, there's no need." Her breathing was heavy. "There's only one little thing," she said.

"What?"

"Buy me something from Kasos's."

Beads of sweat broke out on her forehead again. Her eyes were cold. There was panic in his voice: "I won't leave you alone today. Look at yourself. You're not well."

She smiled. "I'm better now, truly. All I need is a little rest. That's all."

"What did you want me to buy you?"

"Will you?"

"Yes."

"Cigarettes. A pack of cigarettes."

On the low bedside table, next to the reading lamp, he saw the empty teacup. He went over to the window and opened the shutter. A bright light broke in through the window screen. "I'm cold," said Hagar and curled up between the sheets.

"Since when do you smoke?" he asked.

"Perhaps I'll want to smoke when you're not here," she said.

"Why on earth should you?"

She smiled at him. "You said you'd buy them for me."

"I didn't think you were going to ask for cigarettes. Why on earth should you begin smoking now?"

"I heard that cigarettes help you think."

"Are you kidding?"

She drew her hand out from under the sheet and wiped the sweat off her forehead. Her face was yellow. "You're ill, I think," he put his hand on her forehead again. "I'll go and buy you something, but not cigarettes." He went out, and she remained on her own. She heard the hinges of the gate creak and the sound of the jeep backing into the street.

Light pouring into the room woke her up, and she got out of bed and went to the kitchen in her nightgown. She made a salad, an omelet, cut a few slices of bread and spread them with butter. As she was boiling water for coffee she heard the jeep parking in the street. She washed her face and combed her hair. Her face was fresh, but the expression in her eyes was the same. The gleam was gone, they were dull and blank. "You got up?" said Tuvia as he entered the kitchen. Hagar stirred the coffee and said to him: "I told you that I feel fine." But he noticed her hands shaking as she set the cups on the table.

She sat down opposite him. "I brought you pills," he said. "Take them if you don't feel well. And go to bed."

"Why don't you drink your coffee?" she asked.

"So that you can think better," he said, "I brought you the cigarettes too." He put the pack down next to her coffee cup. "Thanks," she said.

She didn't take a single cigarette in his presence. Not till after he left did she get back into bed and snuggle into the sheets. The shutters were open, and she felt lonely and exposed. She was cold. Her legs felt weak. She couldn't get out of bed, but the open shutters bothered her. Her nightgown was soaked with sweat again. The light bursting in revealed her naked. She got out of bed and closed the shutters. Now the room was dark. There was a cup of cold tea on the bedside table, next to the pills and the pack of cigarettes. She took a sip of tea. Then she lit a cigarette. The smoke choked her, and when she wanted to put the cigarette down, she realized that there was no ashtray in the room. Again she had to get out of bed. There was only one ashtray in the house, in the living room. The smoke was choking her. She got the ashtray and on the way she collected the knitting bag too. She coughed and broke into a sweat again. The weakness spread through her body. She put the cigarette into the ashtray and took out her knitting. Beneath the ball of wool were two pages. A squared page, with the knitting instructions on it. And a coarse, unlined page, with pencil writing on it. The soldier's letter. She wanted to read the instructions, but she couldn't see properly. She switched on the lamp. A pale light flooded the sheet. The smoke rising from the cigarette to the yellow lamp collided with the glass and dispersed. She took another puff. The smell of the cigarette brought back the smell of the soldier's sweat and his oil-stained shirt. She knitted. The ticking of the alarm clock merged with the clicking of the knitting needles. She took another sip of tea, put the needles down, and closed her eyes. The lamp, which she had forgotten to switch off, woke her up. She opened her eyes in a panic and heard the ticking of the clock. The cigarette wasn't smoking any more. It had consumed itself, and in the ashtray she saw only a long finger of ash, which still kept the shape of the cigarette. She had stopped sweating. The weakness in her legs too had disappeared. The warmth in which the sheet had wrapped her was now an irritating itchiness. She straightened out the sheet, opened the shutters a little and returned to her knitting. Then she put her hand into the knitting bag. She took out the soldier's letter and read it again. "I waited for you all afternoon. I saw policemen in the vicinity. Did something happen?" Yiftach's fingers crawled up the wall, touched the windowsill. Did he have the canteen with him? How had he managed with the yellow cover she had sewn for it? She dropped the letter and buried her face in her hands. Something stabbed her. She winced and tears came into her eyes. What had happened that day? She wanted to get out of bed, get dressed, and go to Sarah. The pattern of white flowers on her dress ran past her eyes. In the kitchen cupboard were sour candies, and the night when Yiftach had come to ask for a bit of salt came back to her. She dreamed. The soldier's letter lay on her chest. Her eyes were on the ceiling again. Yellow stripes crossed it, coming from the cracks in the shutter. Tuvia had brought her the cigarettes, just as she asked. Why had she asked for cigarettes? She closed her eyes and turned her head to the lamp. The ticking of the clock hammered in her head. Tuvia had gone to Jerusalem. She wanted to hear the sound of the jeep in the street. She looked at the clock. A quarter to eleven. She felt the ashtray with her fingers. She touched the ash of the consumed cigarette. When would he come back? She tried to calculate the times, but the hours got mixed up in her mind. He had said he would come home early. When? The letter was still rustling between her fingers. The clock ticked. The knitting lay on Tuvia's pillow. There was ash sticking to her finger. She was irritated by the sheet wrapped around her but she couldn't get out of it. She pulled the clock toward her and set the alarm to go off at half past three in the afternoon. She wanted to go on sleeping. If he comes back by then, I won't go to the Arab village, she said to herself. And if he doesn't come back? Before she fell asleep she drank the dregs of the tea in the cup. When the alarm went off she jumped out of bed and tore off the sheet. It seemed to her that she had only just fallen asleep. She sat on the bed. It was exactly half past three. Tuvia wasn't back. It was quiet outside, and from far away, like the sound of waves breaking, rose the roar of the crowd at the soccer match. She stretched her arms back. Again she looked at the clock. "I don't believe it," she said to herself. "Another half hour, I'll give him another half hour." She set the alarm for four o'clock and went back to bed.

The distant roaring wouldn't let her sleep. She closed her eyes and lay awake, waiting.

24

The jeep was alone on the road. The sky was blue and empty. A Sabbath morning. Bereft of people.

At one of the junctions soldiers held out their hands to hitch a ride. He drove slowly, undecided as to whether to pick them up, and in the end he stopped. The soldiers got off at Ramla, and he continued on his way.

He met the whole family at the hospital. His sisters, his brothers-in-law, his mother, and his stepfather.

"Where's Hagar?" they asked him.

"She isn't feeling well," he said.

"She never does, when she's got to do something," said Edna. His mother was silent.

"She's a good cook," said his stepfather.

He still hadn't looked at the baby.

Tuvia arrived at the hospital at eleven-thirty, and at one he was already on the way home. Edna had invited him to lunch, but he declined the invitation on the grounds that he wanted to get back to Hagar, who wasn't feeling well.

"But you'll come to the *brit*," said his mother.

"Yes, I hope so," said Tuvia.

And later, casually, he asked: "What are you going to call him?"

"Yehiel," said his mother, "after your father."

"After your father who didn't like Hagar," said Edna, as if to herself.

"Have you got something against her?" Tuvia asked her angrily. "What has she ever done to you?"

"Me?" said Edna. "She hasn't done anything to me. The trouble is that she hasn't done anything to you either."

It was lunchtime. He wandered around the Jerusalem streets. On Jaffa Street he found an open restaurant and went inside to eat. It was a hot day, and before leaving the restaurant he bought himself a bottle of beer.

In the forest next to Hartuv, families were picnicking. He didn't stop for any hitchhikers. He drove slowly and he was afraid to think.

When he reached Tel Aviv he drove to the sea. The beach was full of swimmers, and he went on driving along the cliffs that rose above the white sand, with the sea beating calmly against them. He parked the jeep on a deserted bit of beach where the sea came up to the cliffs and there was no sand to sunbathe on. He sat on a sharp rock and looked at the sea. At the low waves. At the little racing boats. The light breeze dried his back, which was damp with sweat. Suddenly he thought of Bulkin, and he asked himself, where does he get the strength to live alone over there, at the edge of the village? "And you," he asked himself, "aren't you alone now?" Waves broke on the cliff and sprayed white foam. Around the rocks protruding from the water were patches of green slime. A young couple were picking their way between the rocks. He saw them laughing, but he didn't hear a sound. The glitter of the sun on the waves dazzled him.

The couple disappeared and he stood up and returned to the jeep. There were green bushes on the dunes, and when he tried to pluck a twig it pricked him. His shoes filled with sand. There were white clouds in the sky. He looked at his watch. A quarter to four. He had missed the soccer match.

He drove home. He pressed his foot on the gas as if he were in a hurry to meet someone. But he knew that there would be no meeting.

25

A pack of cats ran across the field and escaped into the orange grove. She had a fresh frock on. There were two white ribbons tied in her hair.

The soldier was in fatigues. He hadn't changed for the Sabbath.

"I'm sleeping in the camp anyway," he said.

They wanted to go to the isolated house behind the *moshav* again, but Hagar was afraid of the old watchman.

"I thought you wouldn't come," said the soldier.

"Me too," said Hagar. "I can't do it to him."

"So why did you come?"

She kicked a little stone, and undid one of the ribbons in her hair.

"To tell you," she said.

There were scratches on the blue paint on the wall. The rooms of the house branched out without any logical order. They sat in the central room. The soldier played with her ribbons. Then they wandered through the narrow corridors with their arms around each other, and passed from room to room. Eventually they found a small, dark room.

The coarse material of his clothing touched her face. "Are you cold?" he asked.

"Why do you ask?"

"You're cold," he said. His hands clasped hers.

"Quiet," she said suddenly. Her laughter stopped abruptly.

"What's wrong?" he whispered.

"I heard something," she said.

He left her and went outside.

"I'm afraid," she said. They couldn't see each other in the dark room. Invisible mosquitoes whined. Hagar lay pressed up against the wall. And as she felt the cold floor beneath her back, heavy footsteps clattered into the house.

"The old watchman?"

The soldier didn't answer.

Hagar stood up, and leaned against the wall. The soldier laced up his boots.

"Come into the corner," he said, "no one will see us."

"Yes, they will," said a voice.

"Yes, they will." There was a terrible look on his face. His eyes were big, his hair was cropped, his beard unshaven.

"So you're here?" Hilmi came into the room, into the dark. "Come, come with me." Hilmi's hand was hard. He pulled her after him, and the soldier burst forward, and pulled her away.

"Leave her alone," he cried out loud. Hilmi was pushed to the wall. A grunt broke out of his chest. His head was thrust forward.

"Come," said Hilmi.

She emerged from the dark room and trailed after him, dazed. The soldier followed her.

"Where are you going?" called the soldier.

Hilmi said no more. He stepped between the stones. His feet were steady, but Hagar walked behind him as if in chains, stumbling on the stones and thorns.

The soldier clutched her arm.

"What's the matter with you? Come away from here. Look at his face." The soldier's eyes were panic-stricken. "What's the matter with you?" His voice choked. His hand trembled, and when he took it away, his fingers left marks on her arm.

Hilmi didn't take trodden paths. His sandaled feet were bound in rags. He walked straight ahead. Over thorns, clods of earth, low stone walls.

Hagar took no notice of the soldier and as if obeying an order, she followed Hilmi. Weakness overcame her, and filled her with an inexplicable submission. The soldier too kept quiet, and only once, as if to himself, he said, "Do you know where he's taking us?" He thought that Hagar hadn't heard his question, and he was surprised when she stopped, a bitter smile on her face. "Yes," she said. "You'd better go." But the soldier didn't go. Her strange, remote gaze riveted him to her.

The day was about to disappear. Only the treetops shone. Patches of light and shade dappled the dry ground. Before they entered the orange grove she turned to the soldier again. She was calm. "Go," she said and touched his face. "Go." Her look was soft.

"He might do something to you," said the soldier.

"Don't worry," she said, "he can't do anything to me any more." She bent down and removed a piece of grass that had gotten caught in her shoe.

Hilmi bumped into a branch that barred his way. He pushed it aside, and then let it go abruptly. The branch hit Hagar, walking behind him, in the face, and when they came out of the grove there was a long scratch on her forehead with blood streaming from it.

The trunks of the eucalyptus trees in the army camp were whitewashed. "Are you still here?" Hilmi asked the soldier, who as a last resort seized hold of Hagar's arm again.

"Let's get away from here," he said. "Who knows what he's planning for us. Come on."

Hilmi said nothing. He walked along the fence, and when they came to the gate of the camp, he stopped. "Aren't you going in?" he said to the soldier, and pointed at the tents.

Thorns stuck to Hagar's dress. The scratch on her forehead had dried. They crossed the railway tracks, which were covered with dry branches, and reached an orchard. The fruit trees were bare, the leaves dead. From the orchard a path wound to an abandoned citrus grove, whose fence sagged between bent, broken wooden posts.

Hilmi pointed to the path. "Now," he said, "you go first. But only on the path."

Hagar held her head high. She walked slowly, her eyes fixed on one point. The soldier walked behind her.

There was a splashing sound of running water. A few rows of trees in the grove were still being cultivated. Water ran in the irrigation canals. Green creepers trailed over the lemon trees, and purple flowers laughed among the leaves and the branches which bore no fruit. Next to the running water the path came to an end.

Hagar suddenly bent down, cupped some water in her

hand, and washed her face. The water ran down her dress. She heard Hilmi call: "Cross over, cross the canal. The path goes on."

The cultivated part of the grove ended. Again she was among dry trees, with rotten fruit rolling underneath them. At a short distance from the grove, in a field of thorns, a clump of green bushes stood out like an island.

A bad smell and the neighing of a mule rose from the clump of bushes.

Hilmi ran past the soldier, and Hagar stopped. A stifled cry stuck in her throat.

At first, she saw only the brown belt. Then the yellow material and the silver metal sticking out of it. The canteen.

A piece of black tin lay between the bushes. It covered the mouth of the well. A long sack was spread over the grass, making a little mound. A smell of rot rose in her nostrils. She bent down, and uncovered his face. His face was split. It was eaten by worms. His eyes were closed and drops of water glittered under the lashes. His lips were slightly scratched, and they looked as if they were smiling.

She covered his face with the sack, stumbled and fell on her knees.

"How did he get here?" she said to herself.

Boots smeared with mud flashed in front of her eyes.

"You should know," said Bulkin, whose long hair hung untidily around his neck.

Her hands clutched the damp ground and filled with mud.

"That's enough." Bulkin stepped up to her. "Now go."

"Where to?" she asked.

"To tell her."

"No," she said, "I can't." She wept. "What do you want of me?" she mumbled.

The soldier took a step toward her but Bulkin stopped him. "Enough. Go. Quickly." He pushed the soldier away, out of the bushes.

"I can't, I can't." Hagar writhed on the ground, weeping and scratching herself.

Bulkin lifted her up and stood her on her feet.

"Bring the cart," he said to Hilmi.

The brown mule with the black stripe running down his spine came up to them. He drew the heavy cart behind him.

26

The heat lasted all night. *Hamsin* winds swept the sand, filled the rooms. Nobody slept.

Tuvia came home in the afternoon. The house was in shambles. Old letters were strewn on the floor. Knitting needles were stuck in the pillow. He was hungry. Hagar wasn't home. The clock had stopped at four, when the alarm went off.

He threw the dirty shirts into the laundry basket. He picked up the papers and books. Among the letters he discovered the letter from his sister. He found a page covered with writing in a blunt pencil, in an unfamiliar hand. He folded it up without reading it and put it into one of the envelopes. Hagar's nightgown was in the bathroom, on the floor. Her makeup jars lay open on the marble shelf under the mirror.

The *hamsin* began early in the evening. He took a bottle of cold water out of the refrigerator, went into the living room, and sat down in the dark. He was tired. The tie pressed on his throat. He undid the knot, and opened his collar and the top buttons of his shirt, but he felt no relief. Only the silhouettes of the table, the bookcase, the chairs and the sofa were visible in the hot darkness of the closed room. Suitcases flew before his eyes.

It was night when she returned. She switched on the light, stood in the hall, and sought him with her eyes. He looked at her from the dark living room. Her dress and sandal straps were smeared with mud.

"What happened to you?" He leaped up from his seat.

"Wait," she said quietly, "I'll be back in a minute."

"No," he said, "we have to put an end to this once and for all. What happened?"

He looked at the red scratch on her forehead, and the dried tears with the steaks of mascara they had left on her cheeks. There were thorns sticking to her dress and the white ribbons hung limply in her hair. She went into the bathroom and shut the door. He followed her, tried to open the locked door, and went back to the living room. The bottle of water was empty. He took off his tie, hung it on the back of a straight chair, and sat down in an armchair. His legs were stretched out in front of him. Suddenly he smelled the sea. The smoke of ships in the rain masked his eyes. But outside it was hot and he heard the *hamsin* knocking at the shutters. Knocking, knocking, like his heart.

The splashing of water in the shower stopped and the door opened. With slow, weak steps Hagar came into the living room and turned on the light. She stood in the doorway, next to the bookcase, under their wedding photograph. She was wearing a black dress and sandals. Her wet hair was pulled back, her eyes were naked.

Tuvia rose from his place and Hagar approached him. She stood facing him, and when she met his eyes she said: "There's one more thing I want you to do for me."

"What?"

"Come with me now."

"Where to?"

"To Sarah."

"What for?"

"You'll know everything soon. But I haven't got the strength to go alone."

"Are you all right?" he asked in a weak voice.

The street was empty. They crossed it and stood outside the wooden gate. Sarah and Simcha were sitting in the yard, on low chairs, next to the door of the house. Outside too it was hot and suffocating. Simcha saw them coming, but Sarah said to him: "Go and ask them what they want." Simcha didn't budge from his place. They walked slowly up to him, and Hagar said, "Hello." Only

Simcha replied. Sarah was silent. She sat in her black dress with the white flowers and stared at the sagging fence. Behind her the laundry line swayed in the wind. There was a floor rag hanging from it. Simcha brought two chairs. But Hagar had already seated herself on the high doorstep, opposite them. The chair he had brought for her remained empty.

Silence fell again. Only the wind wailed, and struck their skin. Hagar looked at Tuvia. But he was staring at the ground. Around them was the hot wind and the silence. She waited for a sign. For a can to rattle, a car to pass, a cat's howl to break the silence. She sat on the step and the pale light falling from the light at the front of the house bathed her face. They sat like that the whole night.

Simcha buried his face in his two thick hands. Sarah looked at the fence. She dug her eyes into the barbed wire as if she wanted to get right inside it. The lines on her face were like scratches. Her eyes remained fixed on one spot. There wasn't a drop of sweat on her forehead. Her hands lay on the arms of her chair, her head dropped to her shoulder, and only her hair waved slightly in the hot wind.

The stars were covered with a thick layer of purple haze, and the dense sky seemed about to fall to earth.

It was Simcha's hoarse voice which broke the heavy heat. He pulled a pack of cigarettes out of his shirt pocket.

"You want one?" he asked.

She took one.

Smoke blown from Hagar's mouth, from Simcha's chest, floated on the heavy air. Tuvia didn't say a word.

The wind was hot, and so was the smoke, but Hagar's eyes were moist. "Sarah," she said, "believe me."

Sarah did not avert her face from the fence. Simcha finished his cigarette. When he lit himself another, he asked: "You want another one?" Hagar took the cigarette and rolled it between her fingers.

Tuvia's white shirt was open, and there were sweat stains on the collar. Brown stains which needed laundering. But the laundry line behind her was empty, swaying silently in the wind. Mosquitoes gathered around the lamp which lit the yard. A mosquito hit her forehead, and got entangled in the lock of hair falling over the scratch. The mosquito whined and buzzed in her ear, but Hagar didn't move. In one hand she held the cigarette. Her other hand was on her knee, plucking at the green embroidery which decorated the edges of her dress. Her unmade-up face looked haggard. She looked at Tuvia.

He said nothing. His lips were clamped together. She noticed that he was unshaven. Was that how he had driven to Jerusalem? She didn't recognize his face and she knew that he wouldn't say anything to her. She stood up. Tuvia went on sitting. The wind blew her hair over her forehead.

"Enough," a weak voice suddenly said. "Enough. Go away now." It was Sarah.

The wind blew her dress to one side. Next to the gate she turned around. The three of them looked at her.

The creaking of the gate mingled with the wailing of the wind. Her feet sank into the sand.

27

The next day, at eleven o'clock, the funeral took place. The *hamsin* didn't stop blowing.

Sarah didn't speak to anyone. Early in the morning she took a shower and changed her dress. Because of the strong sun she wore a ragged straw hat over her black scarf. It was impossible to see her eyes. Her face was in shadow.

Friedman the cart-driver passed through the streets with the funeral cart. It was still empty. The wheels clattered over the burnt asphalt and the reins clacked on the horse's hide. The long shafts rattled and the people came out of their houses. The shops along the main street closed, one after the other.

It was hot and a lot of flies collected around the mare's big eyes. There were black tears in her eyes, reflecting the trees and people standing opposite her.

But later on there were no people standing in front of her brown eyes. In spite of the flies swarming round their edges, she held her head up. And behind her, after the long cart, with Friedman sitting on it in his black hat and white beard, walked the funeral procession.

Sarah walked right behind the coffin, close to Simcha, her husband, but not touching him. Her little fists were clenched and blue veins stood out on their rough skin. In the same row walked Tabak and his wife, Kasos and his sons, and the school principal. The pupils were mixed with the crowd. This time they didn't march together. Because of the long vacation, perhaps. Only the wreath-bearers walked in white shirts, in pairs, a boy and a girl.

Tzemach and his partner walked right behind the first row, and only occasionally merged with the grown-ups crowding up behind them.

Tuvia didn't walk with Yoel and Carmela, but at the back, among the people who joined the funeral procession in the street, from the sidewalks, the porches, the storefronts. He was shaved and he wore clean, blue working clothes. The keys of the jeep dangled from his hand.

Bulkin and Hilmi walked behind him. Bulkin was unshaven, and apart from the shabby cap on his head he looked just as he had the day before. In his muddy boots, his worn, brown corduroy trousers. The cap did not succeed in hiding his wild, long hair.

Hagar hadn't come.

"Will you help me take the suitcases to the bus station?" she had asked Tuvia in the morning. She was standing on the ladder and climbing up to the storage loft over the bathroom. There was a bandaid stuck to her forehead, and white powder falling onto her hair. He took the dusty cases from her and put them down on the floor. Out of the corner of her eye she saw him brushing off the dust. "Yes," he said. After that they said nothing. With the help of a sharp knife Hagar tried to scrape the calcium deposits from the kettle. Tuvia went to the funeral alone.

When the procession left the main road and turned onto the dirt track leading through the citrus groves, Bulkin took a long stride and fell into step next to Tuvia. The ground gave off a lot of heat, and the smell of human sweat hung in the air. They didn't greet each other, and Bulkin said: "Go to her."

Tuvia said nothing.

"You can't do much good here. Go to her."

Tuvia didn't say a word, and Bulkin pulled the visor of his cap over his eyes and turned away.

On the right of the road the grove gave way to a plowed field whose high furrows were red, melting in the sun. The old obstacle courses and tall poles dotted about the field reminded him of the distant war, the soldiers' training. Beyond the field stood the school building. It was empty. The pine trees in the schoolyard swayed in the wind, and on the long second-floor balcony the janitor could be seen sweeping the floor.

They took the coffin into the purification chamber. The gravedigger stood between the headstones, next to the hole he had dug. The soil heaped up around the hole was fresh and reddish, and the gravedigger stuck his spade into it and leaned on the handle.

"Bulkin," said Hilmi in a whisper. There was panic in his voice, and he seized Noah by his bare forearm.

Bulkin raised the visor of the cap shading his eyes. "What's happened?" he asked.

"Sarah," said Hilmi. "She's disappeared."

Bulkin took off his cap, slapped his thigh with it, and looked at the people standing crowded together next to the purification chamber building. Old men from the burial society walked among the people rattling tin collection boxes they held in their shaking hands. The coins rang. Hilmi's cropped hair was dripping with sweat, and he ran his fingers through it.

Tuvia stood next to one of the pillars supporting the roof of the purification chamber.

"Go to him," said Hilmi to Bulkin. "You didn't see her eyes."

The stubble of Bulkin's beard glistened with beads of sweat. His black eyes were alert. For a moment his cheeks twitched nervously, then his lips tightened. A mosquito hovered around the rim of his cap, trying to get inside, to the tangled hair.

He looked at Tuvia standing next to the thick wooden pillar. "It's none of our business any more," he said to Hilmi.

Hilmi said nothing. Then he said, "I'm going."

"Where to?" asked Bulkin.

"It's midday, the mule has to be fed."

"Hilmi," said Bulkin, "stay here. It's none of our business any more."

When they took the body out of the purification chamber there was a commotion next to the coffin. Sarah wasn't there. But the heavy heat made the mourners hurry, and afterward it dispersed them.

When the streets were empty Bulkin walked down the main road alone. It was lunchtime. The shops were closed. The wind had died down. Only the heavy heat remained, bowing the dry, gray eucalyptus trees. Bulkin reached the square. He passed Kasos's cafe. Flakes of whitewash fell off the wall onto the paving stones outside. He was hungry, but he didn't go into the cafe. He walked under the ficus trees, turned onto a side path and came to Leibowitz's barbershop.

The barbershop was closed. A white curtain covered the glass door. He climbed the steps and stood on tiptoe. Leibowitz was sitting at the newspaper table and eating. His glasses were lying next to the mirror on the wall.

Bulkin knocked on the door.

"Open up, Leibowitz," he called.

"Who is it?"

He knocked again, and tried to open the locked door. Then he heard footsteps, and the creaking of the key in the lock.

"Ah, Bulkin. This is no time to bother a person." Leibowitz put his glasses on.

"Don't make problems now, Leibowitz. Open up."

Bulkin sat down on the chair opposite the mirror, and Leibowitz put the sandwich he was eating on the table, and wiped his hands on his apron.

"You want me to cut your hair with your hat on?" he

asked in Yiddish. He took Bulkin's battered cap off his head and threw it onto the table.

First he cut his hair, then he shaved him. He lathered his face, and before he reached the upper lip he switched on the fan.

Bulkin looked at himself in the mirror. "You know what," he said quietly to Leibowitz, "leave me a mustache."

"Where will it get you?" asked Leibowitz, again in Yiddish.

"Leave it," said Bulkin. "Why not."

The air in the room cooled. Through the curtains on the barbershop windows and door it was possible to see that outside nothing had changed. Bulkin was already shaved, and Leibowitz washed his face.

After drying the hard skin, he went up to the little cupboard hanging on the wall.

"And what aftershave, Bulkin? Like always? Roses?"

Bulkin stretched his legs out in front of him, leaned on his hand, and looked in the mirror.

"Haven't you got anything else today?" he asked.

"I've got roses. Even chrysanthemums," he said in Hebrew. And in Yiddish he added: "Whatever you like."

There were bits of cut hair all over Bulkin's brown trousers.

"All right," he said. "Let's have chrysanthemums."

A NOTE ON THE AUTHOR

Yeshayahu Koren was born in 1940 in the town of Kfar Saba in what was then British Mandate Palestine. He studied philosophy and literature at the Hebrew University in Jerusalem and is the author of several short story collections. *Funeral at Noon* is his first work to be published in English. He lives in Jerusalem with his wife and four children.

A NOTE ON THE BOOK

The text for this book was composed by Steerforth Press using a digital version of Sabon, a type face designed by Jan Tschichold and first cut and cast at the Stempel Foundry in 1964. The book was printed on acid free papers and bound by Quebecor Printing ~ Book Press Inc. of Brattleboro, Vermont.